PECULIAR PRE-TEENS

PECULIAR PRE-TEENS

PRASHAM MEHTA

PARTRIDGE

To order additional copies of this book, contact
Partridge India
000 800 10062 62
orders.india@partridgepublishing.com

www.partridgepublishing.com/india

ACKNOWLEDGEMENTS

"Feeling of gratitude and not expressing it is like wrapping a present and not gifting it"

the just 'idea' of writing a book was turned into reality by a few special people in my life; The people who have been along with me in this dream catching endeavor. Parents if not because of their efforts, I would have never been able to write this book or be a part of the Milky Way galaxy. Thanks Ma and Pa.

F.R.I.E.N.D.S have been the pillar of support during this entire journey. Thanks a lot Jay for motivating me, thanks Aditya for having faith in me, thanks Kapil. Also, special appreciation for all other friends who have been there to help.

Now the one who turned me from a 'English achi bolne wala' geek into a pro writer – Shimna Maam, thanks for discovering my true potent. Thanks Sunita Ma'am and Principal sir for reviewing the book.

Thanks Shivangee for those amazing doodles. You just added great value to my book. I mean talking figuratively and mathematically; those doodles are really a game-changing factor.

Thanks a lot to Beena Handa Ma'am for adding a silver lining to this book.

Thanks Patridge publications.
Thanks Dhruv
Pooja Fia
Neerav Mama

FOREWORD

Beauty lies in the eyes of the beholder. The same situation, but varied responses. If I extend the same logic to the pre-teens, it is the same child, but experienced differently by parents, teachers and friends. This book-Peculiar Pre-teens – by Prasham Mehta provides an understanding of the thinking and feeling patterns as well as the priorities of children and how these manifest into responses to situations. It also reminds us of the dreams and immense potential children have and how we adults can help them to discover it. The beauty of the book is that it is written by a pre-teen in pre-teen age, with experiences still fresh in the mind and who is still on the way of validating his moments of truth.

Prasham has chosen to focus on friends and life at school, showing how small and big incidents become instrumental in learning about oneself, working out strategies to deal with it, thus accumulating life-skills. For a mature person like me, it provides an opportunity to know about what pre-teens think and feel about themselves, about their world, the prevalent jargons and words and ways of strengthening connect with them. The pleasure and pains of processes like class re-shuffling are excellent case-studies of the dynamics between students and teacher-students. The words like frenemy, rhymes like Ego-Lego and wild imagination and comparisons enhances the pleasure and empathy.

This book is a sublimation of creativity identified by his teachers, encouragement provided by the parents, teachers and friends and the risk and initiative Prasham has taken by sharing his experiences, reflections and lessons learnt from mistakes too! I had a lot of interaction with him when he came to Poiesis three years back, from Surat, for our confidence and aspiration building programs in the summer vacation. As a mentor, it is a great feeling to see his creativity expressed in print. I challenge him to be at his best in whatever endeavors he undertakes and excel in life.

Best wishes for a smile and success, always!

Beena Handa
Founder
Poiesis Achievement Foundation
Ahmedabad

PECULIAR PRE-TEENS

Pre-teen: the most unexpected person on earth. A person with limitless imagination; incredible curiosity; out of the world thought process; hypocrisy in veins and a wicked, amusing and naughty smile. Pre-teens are the most wacky and madcap beings. And the way they are treated is even more bizarre, they are ordered to behave like adults but are expected to live as children.

It's a privilege to cherish the pre-teenage moments. It's the only time when life feels lively and we come across a billion new people, places and things. During this period we get to know about our talents, we find passion in something; we set goals and gradually become a MAN.

Pre-teenage modifies our way of thinking. We pre-teens have a realistic and a bit selfish approach which is sometimes regarded as negative approach. And thus, everyone tries to improve us, so, what we mainly receive from *elders* is the 'ideas' of how to be a gentleman, or the 'habits' inculcated by an effective adult or the 'odds' of us turning into an academic acumen.

This book is about the peculiar pre-teens and their sweet-sour experience of middle school. The experiences described here matter a lot for pre-teens as they influence our passion as well as our payroll; it intensifies our mission as well as our vision. This book is not written by one of those bookish nerds who are complete airheads, but by that undisciplined head who is a prank specialist and a despicable nitwit, so I guess this is gonna be a fun journey.

This book isn't like those classics with a happy ending always, or those emotional climax with artificial tears everywhere, instead this book will be nail biting, giggle creating, jaw dropping (ok, that's exaggeration, I mean this isn't Steven Spielberg writing) book which will surely change the view of the world for pre-teens and also the impression of the world for the world.

Pre-teenage: it's a time when we become the real us, it's when whatever we speak becomes paradoxical. It's a wonderland where every sight is a surprise, it's a forest where every second is breath taking and it's a vacation where every moment is memorable. It's when we understand the principles of adulthood; it's when we undergo the changes of puberty and the time when we grasp the essence of maturity in us.

Being a part of Middle school is like tasting the sourness of life and savoring the tanginess of the real world. It is an endeavor to complete us that is hindered by limitless obstacles that are to be crossed to clinch success. It's when impossibilities increase and for a moment life seems intangible. Every step is an adventure and obscure challenges throng the path. But these difficulties and challenges are the *tadka* of pre-teenage.

During middle school, no one ever stops, everyone briskly walks their path to their goals, and it's just the direction that matters. It's an abyss that is crafted like a modern haven; it's really a wilderness nest.

You enter pre-teenage: you enter social life (actually virtual social life). Pre-teens communicate but they don't talk. It's a sudden change, which leads to gradual development into socialism. Poking on face book starts, the new last closed apps aren't games but twitter and whatsapp and now messaging bills cost parents a big sum of money. Selfies start swarming the SD card.

Life becomes #life. Haha becomes LOL. Apple becomes APPLE iOS8. Show biz becomes the latest lifestyle and criticism becomes an everyday ritual. Here, impression becomes everybody's business and studies are just few hours before the exams. The recesses are a heaven for all pre-teens and usually science is a naptime. Pre-teenage brings a complete change in us, the change that makes us exceptional. It is a radical revolution. It is expectedly unexpected.

This period has no stability; it has limitless upheavals, innumerable ups and downs and infinite twist and turns. The 'downs' come too often but when the 'ups' come we feel as if on the top of the world. The feeling of triumph brings a peculiar satisfaction and teleports us to the cloud 9. But, usually pre-teens enjoy these twists in the tales. Pre-teens love thrill and these upheavals give them a kick.

The worst thing for a pre-teen is to be compared, or get rejected, or be ignored. He can't stand such disregard.

Pre-teenage is when the mind becomes airy and we become airheads. Teenage is said to be a suffocating for parents but believe me pre-teenage is a bigger headache. It's like a high voltage shock for the parents. But sometimes this shock acts like a defibrillator by reviving activeness in parents regenerating their pre-teenage memory. If teenage is said to be a bomb then pre-teenage is a spring trap, it can pop anytime.

Pre-teenage is when relationships grow and freedom increases. It's those golden times when last benches give the feeling of a Mercedes and the first benches are like a bicycle: no matter how much you pedal, you always STAY behind the Mercedes. Pre-teenage is a time of endless gossips, roguish night stays, drowsy science periods and non-stop arguments. It is also the time when we understand the importance of friends and teachers who create the lush green avenue to provide us cool warmth helping us to step into gear and xlr8 to those roads leading to success.

My pre-teenage was really splendid. It had unlimited adventures and escapades. Insanity flowed through our blood and discipline was something impossible. I was really a nutcase. My jokes were pretty awesome and my ego was normal. Alike every unique pre-teen, I was a fun loving and prank creating person.

My experiences of middle school are very complex yet interesting, very idiotic yet meaningful, very humorous yet serious. This book has those memories about my pre-teenage that are just too amazing. Join me on this breathtaking journey amidst my pre-teenage and relate your life with it. I am sure we might get a many similarities. Because, no matter how much we try to be the nerds, no matter how much we follow our parents' suggestions, no matter how much 'goodboy' we try to be, the pre-teenage serum will be always there in each of us.

Now, talking about this book. This book is compiled from those memorable *events* that has happened to me and my friends and how we reciprocated them. This has all those 'to forget' and 'to remember' days of my life. And this book is by peculiar pre-teens, for peculiar pre-teens and of peculiar pre-teens. Here we go... Into the life of a peculiar pre-teen. Find your pre-teenage in it, find yourself in it. So, pre-teens please enjoy reading this book, because your face is the world's future identity, your mind make-up is development that is going to take place, and of course your uniqueness is going to be the beauty of this world. Seatbelts-on.

DAY 1 - EXCITEMENT and THE JUMBLE RUMBLE

The vacations had now ended and sixth grade now rolled. That day, I remember, that the weather seemed pleasant, the atmosphere was fresh as the sun shone bright with clouds to galore the sky, the bus (for a change) was clean and the guy sitting beside was talking for the first time something sensible otherwise he would talk real crap. But all these weren't something special and didn't excite me. The real adrenaline rush was given by the exhilaration of the re-opening of school.

We all reached the class, sat on our benches; we had met after a long time. Two minutes into the class, I started chatting with my friends, talked with them about what we did during vacations and then we started staring at those typical frenemies, and those rivals and all others whom we envy. But the only thing that thronged everybody's mind was about reshuffling. Re-shuffling is a kind divide & rule; the only change is that only the teachers rule, and we don't. It's the system of separating all friends into different sections. It's like a slaughter. Every year, re-shuffling seems exciting, but somehow it turns out to be devastating.

The main reason behind re-shuffling is not to get you known to other people but to decrease the madhouse created by students. If lesser friends be in a class, the discipline level increases. After two years of togetherness, we students were really too close and thus, our pranks were more, gossips were louder and laughter was unstoppable. In short, our wilderness would turn the class upside down. Our fifth grade class was near the small forest area, so while it was calm like a sea in the jungle outside; inside the class, it was a wild and ugly jungle with students playing, girls gossiping, teachers shouting, benches banging, switch boards breaking, pens getting lost, books getting stolen and all. Due to such signature movements, our class was given the title of FISH MARKET ASSOCIATION (FMA).

The current atmospheric wilderness in the class was accompanied by a scent of suspense. Who would go where? That was the question disturbing all minds. But something kept me away from this forest; all I did was remembered the magic moments of the last grade. Like the crazy moments of recess; the naughty talks with friends; the *nicha dikhana* talks with the competitors; the igniting rage talks; the talks of adulation with the class teacher; and also the senseless talks with besties. All pre-teens must have had such moments, remembering old memories gives rejuvenation. Thinking of old days gives satisfactory entertainment (actually more!). People should cherish them. And one should never forget the pre-teenage moments as they make you feel lively even if you are lonely.

Everyone was busy exchanging phone numbers, filling slam books, crossing fingers, and hoping to find all friends in the next class (ain't happening), girls were talking about other class teachers and grading them (gen-next, children grade elders!!), boys were crafting new pranks and other tricks to disturb teachers and complaint boxes and make them go really nuts, but I was completely out of this business, it's logical to do so. Because being into this rubbish gives nothing in return. So I was with my class teacher and having the last conversation. I gave her my feedback, took hers' and talked about all changes she brought in me.

Adulation- that's flattery, it is one of the most powerful things in the world of pre-teens, every pre-teen must have a friend who would always focus on flattery; More than studies or pranks. He has excellent skills in adulation. Even I had a friend and his name was Nikhil, and he only had advised me to do the feedback thing with the teacher. It was a great experience. This Nikhil was known as the godfather of flattery in my class. He could flatter even the toughest guys, the way he looked into their eyes and they just teleported as if in his mind, 'gone'. It was like hypnotism. Plus, he had the fair look, lean body, quick legs, blue eyes. That's all you require to become the godfather, I guess. Apart from flattery skills, this guy Nikhil was smart, cool and sassy. He was good in studies, good looks and had nice topics to speak on. the only flaw in him was that he had this 'ego'.

So in the conversation, the teacher was giving me tips about seventh grade; about middle school to be precise. Tips to concentrate well and work hard, in academics as well as activities. Guidelines to leave no stones unturned, to shine like a star, to be the friendliest, and of course, the methods to adept to the middle school environment well. Those tips, I am sure, would be handy and would help me past the middle school labyrinth. She also suggested me of being on the ground and having no ego. Having such tips, I guess worries won't stand a chance in my middle school journey. Then, after our talk, she stood up with a paper in her hand, adjusted her spectacles and asked me to go back.

The moment arrives!! Eta: 0 minutes. Timed it perfectly, because the students had started losing the zeal, but this small movement, brought back the enthusiasm. With enthusiasm, tension also arrived. The fish market association had become livelier than ever. And then, the teacher shouted and ordered everyone to stay quiet and sit. Everyone did sit, but me, for some reason wandered in the class asking for an eraser (god knows why!!).

"Roll no: 1- 6th D" said the class teacher. Here it starts **THE SEGREGATION.** And one by one, she called out everyone's name, and the division of class had started. After everyone got segregated; few girls who were not with their friends turned cranky. They behaved as if this parting was the end of the world. This separation wasn't a sad and permanent one and it wasn't as if they weren't going to meet afterwards, but girls are girls and melodrama is their surname. So the sobbing started, with their faces frowned as if on someone's death. And for us boys, it was 'never mind'. We had that 'doesn't matter' attitude, the maximum we did after this parting was to decide our next sleepover and also discover a way to meet in the recess. Before getting to know who was going to join me from my old class, I calculated the average. 41/5 (total student / number of sections in 6th), which means that almost 8 students would come with me, that fact gave me real satisfaction as I would get at least 8 known faces, but when I again did the math again, in a deeper way, the aftermath gave me great astonishment. i.e. 41- 20 (girls) - 5 (frenemies) – 3(competitors) – 2 (rivals)= 11. That's too less, the average decreased to 2 friends per class which was hell too less. Now that fact dazzled me. With the minus points, there were also some plus points. It was a mixed group of people.

No besties... Huge reason to worry!!!

No rivals.... I am happy and everybody knows it!!!

No complaint boxes... I can already see the cloud nine.

Clap slap* *clap* *slap* for the teachers. They had done the best they could in the worst way possible. It was an 'okay-okay' shuffling for us. Everyone wants to be with the same friends forever but the sad truth of middle schooling is that teachers hate it.

So with no rivals and no complaint boxes, I was happy, but the one big drawback was that there was no bestie in it. Our gang of 5 dumbasses was completely separated. Broken into pieces; shattered like glass. But I don't guess our friendship would be affected and it would last as long as day is followed by night. Our group was good in studies but with the chaotic behavior we were like outlaws of school. And I guess our disobedience led to the separation of us into different classes. School had done sorcery and put us in a hoax. I am sure this parting will reduce the partying. Without best friends, I thought I would be doomed, with just tolerance and patience to my rescue. And of course, accompanied by loneliness and boredom.

But that's okay, survival wouldn't be 'hard' if I don't have friends, and I can make new friends. On the happier side of parting, I was really happy that there were no rivals from my class. Being with friends gives happiness, but not being with enemies gives additional glee. So that gave me extra hopes of finding new friends in my new class. All rodent-like rivals, cat-like competitors and frenzied enemies were dumped into some other class and that made me feel ecstatic.

That's it. THE END OF SHUFFLING; the end of the jumble rumble of students. And also the dawn of a new class with a whole new lot of students. The seven children who were going to accompany me are down below.

#1 A book worm that would have those very thick glasses. She was a fact fanatic, always filled with resources, but her stammering problem with such boring topics to speak, gave her the name 'buffer stock'.

#2 A punk who would always bunk social studies period and had a tattoo on his belly which he wouldn't show anybody. Abhishek Shah, one of the many rebels from our grade. He always used to feel that he was better, bigger, and elderly than others. But apart from all that, he could bring entertainment, so I felt that his company could be just what I needed to get refreshed.

#3 AN animal lover who would bring all kinds of nat geo videos on snakes and vulnerable species. Poorvang Shukla. The most annoying, childish idiot who would fancy catching spiders and watch chameleons change colour. In my opinion, he was a snake himself.

#4 A simpleton who would behave nicely with everyone and did not have bad blood with anybody. Nivid Kher, my only friend on the list. Mediocre, meticulous, and an accountable man, he was.

#5 A crazy sportsperson who would always wear shorts inside his pants, just in case anybody called for basketball auditions.

#6 A daydreamer who would always want to sleep, and would snore real loud during science period. She would always get lost in the depths of neverland, I suppose. Just playing with her hair, with eyes looking at the ceiling and legs moving in jazz. Her name... um.... I don't actually remember. We would usually call her by the name 'krimasourus'.

#7 A grumble machine that really was jealous of my attitude and personality and just couldn't bear me. She was indeed too immature, envying me always. Often she found some stupid reasons just to prove me arrogant or shameless or unworthy. Unfortunately fortunate, her efforts usually went in vain.

These were the people from my class and at that moment, we were also accompanied by anxiety and curiosity to know whom else from other class would accompany us into this new endeavor.

At the end, the shuffling seemed to be just the contrast of what I wanted. During pre-teenage, everything that happens is either unexpected or sudden, and this change was a combo pack. The atmosphere during that shuffling was like a nightmare. I had the idea of having it boisterous and active, but it turned out to be as dead quiet as a graveyard. Everyone seemed to be spellbound as the shuffling just bewitched everybody. ***Shocked***. ***Traumatized***.

'Line up' said the class teacher. Her third instruction that day and maybe the last one from her as our class teacher. As we all started lining up, packing our bags, collecting everything, and having a last look on the soft board we decorated, the class was turned upside down. Before, the class was tranquil, like a calm Sunday morning at the beach, and then it suddenly changed into a Friday night pub. It had again become the fish market association. I packed my bag, stuffed those thick textbooks and all new notebooks, and then caught hold of my bottle that was hidden by one from our group, returned the eraser and went straight to the gate.

It seemed as if no one was happy, and everyone wanted to rumble about the jumble; grumble about the grouping; complain about the classification.

ADIOS! YA AMIGOS

As the five lines started moving, looking as the distributaries of a river, the situation really turned dramatic. And then, out of nowhere, I just yelled 'adios', just to thank everyone for being with me for those two special years, and biding adieu to them by wishing luck for the following year. Girls went physically emotional and boys were sad but wouldn't show it. The bond of 2 years was broken by a game of 20 minutes.

Everyone had already started missing their friends, their enemies, the double dholkis. Nevertheless, everything flowed normally like water and it ought to because no one could change what had happened, so they had to adept and move on. With that in mind, everything went normal, smooth until the last minutes.

Last minutes have always been terrible for us humans. We Homo sapiens have the habit of forgetting something really important and they get the knowledge of it during the last minutes. This syndrome is in our nerves. And this is one of the only genes common in all humans.

So the same thing acted upon me and as it clicked me, I started questioning myself. "What was it that I had forgotten? Had it be relating the new class? Had it be relating my old enemies?" I asked myself. On getting no clue on what I had forgotten, I asked myself, "Oh boy, why don't I remember it? Am I suffering from retrograde amnesia? Or is that I am lost?" Lots of questions!! No sign of an answer, still with great conviction, I said to me "I will find what I have forgotten in a jiffy". This conversation between me and me was seriously dumb and it looked nerdish but was coming to me on its own.

I mean not literally a jiffy. Because that would be like 1/1000th of a second or a zero here and there. What I actually meant was to find the answer quick. Then the inner voice came up with the probable options and suggested me: Had I forgotten to take the phone number of the class teacher? I don't think so; had I forgotten to show my jumping hiddles (eyebrows) to my friends or the girls around? Not at all.

"'Friends' holy cow!!!" the tube light inside my brain just flashed. OMG. I had forgotten to wish my best friend luck for the next year; I had forgotten to say him a good bye in our style. This might sound too kiddish, but if you all go to your pre-teenage, I am as sure as death that you might have some special interactions with your friends and also would have some unique kind of saying good bye. This thing was very crucial for me. It could not be left undone.

Plus, that friend was very special for me. Jay Desai, his name. He was happy-go-lucky and straight forward and an all-rounder. He looked innocent on the outside but in reality he was another misfit in the room. We had played too many pranks together. Tall and stout, a younger version of GRU from despicable me. His hair were as if stunned by electric shock and had a mark on the lower right side of his cheeks.

People have special ways of biding adieu to their besties. Like a different kind of handshake, a hug, a wink, a naughty smile with skeptical expressions. It can be anything and everything. It should just be special and from heart, because that's what matters in friendship. Yup! Everyone would be having their 'specially patented' style of greeting friends.

I just dashed to my friend, and to that, even he realized this missed action. Our style was completely nuts. It was just too berserk, too crazy, and too pre-teenish. Girls got disgusted from it and boys appreciated it. It was wickedly different. The thing was to shake hands like gentleman, give a straight look into the eyes and then just kick on the butt too hard. Endless gigs then followed this. It was really awesome. Like soda, damn cold and fizzy. We called it 'The After-Shock'. One sec. who's 'we'? Well, 'we' is our gang, the 'formal badasses'. We group of four. Jay, Aditya, Kapil and me. They were my guides, my friends, and my companions. In short, my treasure at school.

Now, I was relieved, satisfied. And was also ready for any change to occur. Now was the time to wash the past, and create a new folder for the future.

Adios ya amigos! They had given me so much. I owe them (but its okay to be in debt with them). The moments I had cherished with them, the smiles, the anger, the rage, the slaps, the claps, the laughs, the talks, and all those times when we rocked. jay, as I told you was the simplest guy I had met and he was the one who knew to give me a flight whenever I learned something new, and also knew how to prick my balloon whenever I went too high (ego), helping me fall back on the ground. Aditya was the one who put hurdles in my path to teach me how to leap. Kapil was the one who would give up parties for our stupid sleepovers. Pre-teenage is a time when life becomes friends and friends become life.

Cheerio! Adios! Hasta la vista! Au revoir! Good-bye! Sayonara! A good bye in all languages is for those who understood the language of my heart. But, I don't get it, why is everybody and I getting so dramatic? This change has not broken but strengthened our bonds and we are going to meet each other during recesses or bunks or parties. So chill.

Every pre-teen should enjoy these small moments, because they give eternal and internal happiness. And they should care for friends. Live in the small moments, they help you laugh even during greatest of your problems, they make you able even when you feel that you are the weakest, they make you cry even when you feel like the king of the world. The small moments emotionalise your life. They grease the different activities of your life.

THE NEW CLASS

After leaving the class, with just those funny memories, we walked down to our new class hoping to make new friends. I was having nostalgia, remembering Aditya saying, "Make new friends but always remember the besties". Then I finally reached my new class.

The location of the class was pretty lousy. It was at the extreme corner of the left wing, so basically far from everywhere: washrooms, stairs, and other classes even. The only good thing about the class was that it was far from all disturbances, no yelling, or shouting, no rush in the corridor and it seemed to be a peaceful class.

I entered the class, with an half-smile, glittery eyes and my hands over the straps, for a second my body became just numb because of the whole smothering atmosphere, but a push from some idiot kid just teleported me back to the real world.

And then, I just had a 'peek-a-boo' over my new class and the people in it. But for some reason, I just couldn't recognize anybody. I had seen them before but couldn't recall the names. What was it? I mean, it felt as if I was in some other world. Had anybody deleted the 'c' drive off my brain?

The first job I needed to do was to find friends, new friends. The first one was Ritesh, who was with me during the annual sports day the previous year. He was a menace, like me, which would suit me just perfectly. So, I sat beside him. He talked too much. Long hair, short face, blue specs and those naughty eyes. He was resourceful, amiable and trustworthy. A night can be without stars but he cannot lie.

The next guy I spotted was the twin brother of one of my bestie Mrutyunjay, which meant he would be having the same attributes and attitude. His name of Mahipal, but after the day I met him, I called him mad nut. He was pretty good, a bit knowledgeable and of course kick ass talented. I would call those twins 'RANA facsimiles' as their head name was RANA. Both brothers looked same like Zach and Cody. They were fair, cute like rabbits and damn sharp. One twin was a mathemagician while other was an experimentalist. But both were true mentalists and could provide nice company.

I was certainly overwhelmed by getting so many new friends. Next friend I just dappled was Keshav who was with me during a party; he was a simpleton but fun loving, so I befriended him right away. He had this crazy love for video games and liked to do duty, Angry young man like a commander.

Finding friends right away gave me delight. And at that time, middle school felt normal though middle school is normally abnormal. With friends on my side, I was ready to face any heat.

And after that, I looked upon all other people of the class; the class was not at all bad. The girls were not hyperactive with short temper, no rivals, and everyone had that supportive and amiable nature.

Oh! I had forgotten about the class teacher. We were going to face a strict class teacher. Everyone was afraid of her. She was terrible. Her anger was danger for students. Stern, stringent and just too horrific. OMG!!

I mean that everyone calls her mean. Students even grade her. That's terrible, to grade teachers are like grading people who are far more superior and educated then us. We aren't as qualified and sensible as critic and we have no knowledge of diplomacy and perspective and tactics. Still some morons have to criticize teachers. But the way they ranked the teacher gave me scares. They said she was too stringent and could not withstand misfits (that's me).

I was very popular amongst the seniors, and that's good because their friendship makes decision making a lot easier. They give precise, concise and right tips that help taking the right turns at the right moment.

So, they gave me considerable information about the teacher and the way they told me gave me Goosebumps. They warned us about the strictness of the teacher and also the things that annoy her. If we see, from teacher's point of view, they have done it perfectly, placing that teacher in our class. Because I guess, she's the only one who can 'control' us.

We pre-teens have the mind-set of getting paranoid by someone strict. It can be a friend who just wants to get u back on track, to remove your ego; or it can be a parent wanting you to grow more, learn more; or it can even be a teacher wanting you to get more simple and down to earth. So, first, I thought she would be like one of those, scolding necessarily.

But, the way the teacher turned up to be was just the contrast. Ever heard of an orthodontist? The one who breaks or straightens your teeth, well, this teacher was like one of those. She would be waiting to break or straighten one's ego. That's a big flaw, because I have EGO.

I thought that if I made a good relationship with the teacher, then my pre-teen life would be set. Because if she troubleshoots my mischiefs, I wouldn't have that notorious name, which would be good. But if she does that by spanking, than I might be in a mess.

I got a pretty good class with new friends, and all good people around me; the only thing that worries me is the orthodontist. As of course, I ain't ready for a denture. But by the tips of the seniors, all I can guess is destruction of ego by the teacher, in a explosive manner.

After going under a social change, we pre-teens get saddened, disheartened. Our life feels miserable. And we feel lonely and unwanted. And this change had a critical effect on us. But what I think is that old is gold but new is raw. You ought to polish it to find its real value. Pre-teens must forget his old possessions and get obsessed with what the new things.

And that day I decided firmly that I wouldn't cry in the old memories of the past but will embark like a brave man on this new journey to make my nice relationship with the teacher. It might be too tough, but b-t-w which pre-teen likes easy jobs?

THE REPULSIVE RESPONSE
OF THE CLASS TEACHER

I had adapted to the class and was really enjoying it. New friends brought jokes and charm to the class. The co-operation of class gave high scopes of laughter, giggles, or, as the new gen says, LOL and ROFL and hehe.

But as the teacher revealed her real prowess of strictness, things changed. She turned into a real orthodontist (ortho-egoist) that hindered our chuckles. Her anger was so powerful that it could bring nuclear strike like in Hiroshima, in Switzerland, or could start the French revolution in the democratic republic of Congo out of nowhere. She was rather an excellent social studies teacher but also one big hell of a stern figure. And her orthodox 'don't spare the rod' methods just started.

The first day, Mahipal got insulted, he was called a mouse and was shown the eyes, eyes of anger. That heat was too much and just created a big fear. And the other day, it was Ritesh's chance to get insulted.

Strictness could be handled by us pre-teens, because every person elder to a pre-teen tends to scold him. We are habituated for spankings from our parents or teachers, or big brothers or any damn elder and the main reason behind it is just because we are too curious and creative; just because our imagination rules some other horizons.

But, a teacher or anybody for that matter, insulting a pre-teen is just unbearable. And that too, just because the perception is different than some average mediocre people. Optimism depends on your perspective, one might take things in another way, that doesn't mean he is a nut case or maniac. A half empty gun would anyway give less mental stress than a gun half full. Even though, they are the same thing, just represented in a different way. Why talk about some stupid glass every time and select the half full option as more fruitful and optimistic. Think different.

So, because my thinking was different, that didn't mean I was completely nuts. I had a different outlook to the world, but the teacher thought I was just an egoistic idiot gone bananas. And I would feel "grow up, ma'am, if everyone starts thinking same, I guess it would be a robotic world". And her orthodox thinking was accompanied by her habit of calling everybody with obnoxious name. and that's a big insult. This ain't done.

Attitude is something relative. It is never good or bad. It is and should be unique not ubiquitous. What really matters is the perspective. Changing attitude is just like boiling or freezing water, no matter how many forms it changes, its composition remains the same and it returns to its actual position eventually. the pressure of flame or the force of chloro-fluoro-carbon (main gas of the refrigerator) wouldn't be able to change its chemical properties, i.e. the root properties.

Her insulting everybody just set off everyone's mood. We pre-teens can't handle so much of such repulsive response. Repulsive response is like the last thing a pre-teen would want. Actually second last. The last being.......Ummm.... Not now!!! She wanted to run a revolution, an ego removing revolution which might feel the right thing to do unless the way of doing be so disgracing and disgusting.

So those insults basically demoralize a pre-teen. And that's what become the reason of all frustration, and the thwarting of a person that works as a weapon to smother himself/herself. Plus the irritation, and the stress at the temple. I mean, self-respect is also important, right? Someone can't just insult you in front of your newly made friends, or other competitors or people of another sex, or someone who expects to hear all praises about you.

Every pre-teen loves to doze on the respect recliner. But here, everything was anti-respect, anti-esteem. A class teacher should be a role model, parent-like. But from the current situation, all I can say is that the class teacher is a paranoid predator.

No doubt about her S.S. teaching. She could teach history very well, and not make it boring with all those interesting examples and stories but here again, she would upset me. she hated my sense of humour, and I had a vast joke list that I would play during the most serious times during the social studies period.

I was really in a fix here, in loophole, because this teacher was just too much for me to handle. Her insult would pierce everybody's heart and those obnoxious names can just demoralize each and every peculiar pre-teen.

The relationship between a teacher and a student has always been special as it matters a lot. Every pre-teen needs to have a teacher enlighten him. To print a success story, pre-teens need to find the right teacher, the right inspiration. Pre-teens should find some perfectionist teacher to inspire, because after every excellent person is a childhood mentor.

Something has to be changed, because me or even any other pre-teen cannot digest insult, and cannot intake such repulsive response. At that moment, we thought that either the teachers need to consult some softhearted spirit. Or she has to find someplace other.

And it wasn't like that that we never tried to try her methods, impress her. We did. Ritesh and I designed a card, keshav brought some Bengali sweets and a rose while I asked abhishek to prepare a sweet speech. But she did not liked it, she said that she couldn't be 'flattered'.

I couldn't understand what was with her, I mean was she into something else, was she lonely, was she expecting something else from us, was she just trying to stay away from us? Who know?

Humans cannot handle people who don't listen to them, and mark them as enemies or simply as people whom the don't 'care' about. And that's natural, supposedly that happened with me, I judged the teacher without even thinking through her kaleidoscope. And maybe that's why I and maybe every human finds it hard to accept differences. In a way, the teacher was also wrong, but I was 'wronger'. So friends, learn this important thing, that everything that glistens is not gold, vice versa. It could be that inside this hard oyester there might be a pearl hidden. Find it. But....

100% SURE, THE GRASS IS GREENER ON THE OTHER SIDE

In the English language, there lies a proverb 'grass always seems to be greener on he other side' (this might be helpful to pre-teens in the writing section during exams!!), that maxim means that we humans never get satisfied with what we have and always think that others have it better. For a century or more, many legends have preached, many elders have repeated abut this and said that's its completely true, they say that this proverb is an idea of how human mentality is.

But for us pre-teens, things are always different. For us pre-teens, this proverb is not applicable every time, there are times when someone else is really luckier. In reality, for pre-teens, everything happens in the most unlikely manner, in the most contrast manner than prescribed in those 'wisdom words'. Grass is sometimes greener on the other side and there are a lot of scientific possibilities to it, like if the grass sown is low quality than the other side, or if the stout sheep have rout the grass and there's no roots left whereas the other side is crowded by slender goats having poor appetite, or if the soil is overused and the nutrients are just too low than the other side.

So, during a pre-teen's life, such situations come a many time, like when you come with a new watch in the class and the one whom you envy the most comes with a more classy and expensive watch catching everybody's eyes and just dumping our watch into the ditch. Or when you have to plead for just a soft toy for hours and your archenemy gets a whole new Xbox. And at those times, we really can feel the greenery on the other side.

Jay rushed towards me and told me about his class teacher. And then I was just numb. With eyes wide, mouth open, and my double chin looking as a chump. The reason being the CLASS TEACHER.

While we got a stern class teacher, my nemeses, or those dorks that had bad blood with me, and even my bestest of friends got the best class teacher one could ask for. A modest genius, a kind virtuoso (some word from thesaurus meaning genius). Perfect for me or any pre-teen. She was liked by all pre-teens: nerds, geeks, dweebs, dorks, average students, chaotic students, straight A's students, all-rounders, sport freaks; all kind of people like her.

That teacher would interact and resolve the problems of students like a parent does, and would enjoy the small moments of happiness with the children like siblings. She was more like a friend who enlightens than a teacher who makes us mug the textbook completely. She shows the right path to everybody, motivates the slow-learners, teaches modesty to the smarty-pants who are getting a bit ego. She is the ideal teacher everyone should get. Perhaps, she might not be a legend, but she is truly a person who will inspire others to grab success and become a legend.

So giving them THAT and us THIS is completely unfair. It's like ornamenting them with gold and asking for satisfaction by giving us some cheap brass. Our teacher being away from laughter and giggles, she looks like an investigating officer, always skeptical about her students. Whereas, on the verified greener side, the class teacher has complete faith and trust in us students.

Our teacher refrains us from talking and being more social and is damn too particular about homework submissions, discipline and taking responsibilities. While the better one believes in 'living in the today' thingy.

It is out of comparison. Undoubtedly, the other teacher is better. No disputes. She is more lenient and understands us pre-teens perfectly. She can grasp the misfit behavior and reciprocate accordingly. She understands the requirement of the round pegs in square holes and knew the stupidity reckoned by a nerd who reads 24/7.

After knowing the sad truth, I was feeling jealous of the other class lying on the greener side. Not only the greener side, I guess they had a porch, a well and a functioning irrigation system. So, that's just too much more superior than our barren land.

This might happen with every pre-teen in his/her life and this is what adds that bitter punch to the life mélange. We wish to get the best resources but end up having either great expectations or hard luck. We want to get trained from the best teacher, want to be accompanied by the best of friends and want our life controlled by the kindest of the Gods!!! but always end up having boring teachers, frenzied friends, fanatic gods and an abnormally normal life.

So now, in my class, we had to be like slender goats as the grass was far too less, i.e. the moments with smile on the orthodontist were almost nil. So now in my class, freedom of attitude and liberty to laugh was forbidden. As we had become humanoids (human + android). Or actually more apt word is puppets, real puppets that could do just as much as the string could be stretched and would go as high as the controlling hand would want us to go. Whereas in the greener side, on the wonderland it was like your world. Do as it pleases. Turn the damn class into a circus or a zoo or a fashion studio, nobody denies or interferes. It is like living the dream by getting a seat n that classroom, a dream in the insight of every pre-teen, and what we got to endure was a nightmare.

What really hurts me is the fact that the previous year I did all the flattery and nothing's been paid off. The other classmates who got to go on the greener side have never given a thank you note or a card or anything that fancies a teacher, and still they make it. School one will have to clear my debts, but when?

And another astonishing fact is that the other sections also have got a considerably better and less enraged class teachers. So that means my flattery was no good or that this is someone's conspiracy. And I am really sensing something fishy. I pedaled the whole year, and they get the BMW. It's like my sweat and their seat. Huh! I am furious.

The axiom has been proved wrong. This means that life is not about being philosophical but realistic. I am 100% that we are getting dried, dehydrated and juiceless hay and the other side getting fresh, juicy and green grass (in abundance). It is like I am isolated on an isle that is a labyrinth of strictness itself. But I am not going to act scaredy like an ostrich that would bury his head all into the sand hoping that the predator would vanish, I will, with my shoulders straight and chest out, face this challenge which is entangling me. I will try my best to pull through this problem and am going to face it with courage. Pre-teens should never lose hop and never jeopardize their courage.

Keeping cool, I will try making myself more disciplined and organized. It isn't an extreme adventure, for which I need to become Bear Grylls, it is just pre-teenage. I want to turn up as a triumphalist in the eyes of every visionary of school, in the hearts of every friend and in the speech of every orator of school.

So, tolerance it shall be.

This class teacher gave us a lesson. That's to expect the unexpected every time in middle school, you never know what destiny decides or what verdict it writes, or what follows my acts. All we need to do is keep calm, stay quiet, adept well and get our Goosebumps petrified.

REALISING THE SOFT SPONGE
INSIDE THE HARD SHELL

The school started working, it was functioning alright, there were the same old lame complications with the class teacher, and we all were studying because we could do nothing else.

But then something happened. Sometimes a person might be too harsh from outside but soft inside. Sometimes a person is different and we should not judge them from the way they react. Sometimes people take the 'spare the rod and spoil the child' protocol too seriously.

Pre-teens should not count them as ruthless jerks, or stern beasts but as those special people who want to be harsh on us just to make us down to earth and adapt to the realistic and simple behavior. These people are like radicals and they have a huge impact on how our world works.

While we were trying to get rid of the repulsive response, thinking as if we were Avengers, and trying to overcome the insults she made; precisely, talking about her brutality, she was cooking something else in her mind. Something with unique ingredients and just delicious aroma.

Besides her routine insulting, and the hindering us by barricading our pre-teenage and scraping our smiles off our faces, she had some thinking going on inside her mind. Some little crafty special different idea. That planning was making me unusually curious and a bit skeptical.

And lo and behold, she suddenly wanted to confront all of us and then gave us a sudden shock by prompting an idea too tremendous. She asked us too organize a small party in the class before summer break rolls. Wow. I and Mahipal were stunned, and Nikhil almost fainted. I mean how is this possible. She and a party? You must be kidding me.

Now that's a change, a modification. Is she really the class teacher that felt as a sac of stress? Or is this just another lame joke? Or is this some kind of dream you get after watching some comedy animation film by Pixar? Because that was completely out of syllabus, out of the book, out of my and every classmates' imagination. It ain't a dream, I realized that as soon as I pinched myself from my stunned hand that were almost shivering. It was a dream come true and that too from a so-called creator of nightmares for pre-teens.

Being stern does not mean one can't plan a party, everyone is funaholic. Everyone was just delighted. So, then we realized that the one who scolds with those big scary eyes, and creepy facial expressions doesn't mean they are evil or bad or even a demon it just means that they want us to be perfectionist and for that they use such weapons. Their intension ain't bad but the intensity of rebuking was.

44

You know! Such kind of people, that are hard on the outside like a shell, completely enraged and covered with disgust and anger, and soft on the inside life a sponge, sweet and meticulous and stoic. Similar like a coconut.

As she gave the idea of party, everyone got engrossed in planning for the party, what theme would it have? What food scheme would be apt? what games would be played? And all such questions. Mahipal suggested bringing all pop and rap songs to class and play them loud with chilled Pepsi and our routine tiffin boxes, too that obviously, the girls did 'eew' and 'gross'. Another guy gave an idea to call some pizza chain, and stuff onto few slices of pizza (with added cheese), at the same time watching some sci-fi movie; the response of the girls was again the same.

Then came the amazing idea of having a fancy dress party, it felt amazing to me and I also decided that I would wear Frankenstein on the party day, but the idea had to be ruled out because we were pretty sure that the school wouldn't give the permit.

Still we hadn't got that perfect idea that we would base our theme on. Everyone, with the party fever, was engrossed in finding something new, kick-ass and fun. We wanted a party where we could rock like anything and go just bananas. The atmosphere was really charged up that day, charged with positivity, energy, zeal, and all those words we find synonymous to enthusiasm in the Thesaurus.

After checking up with the coordinator, and asking for all the permits, and getting a few no's, we finally decided to have a small classroom party with just small arrangements. And we had to do that because that was the only thing that would fit the school norms.

It was decided, our class was divided into four groups, and each had to bring some specific dish. The first group had to make sandwiches, the second was assigned with cake, the third with pastas and the last one had to bring the fiery *khaman dhoklas,* a Gujarati delight.

On the day of party, we all had fun, real fun. Intense fun. But the boys went too crazy, crazier than ever. They sneaked in Pepsi in some way and than gulped it like boozehounds drink. Keshav went nuts on seeing the food, he just dappled everything his eyes could see, and Nikhil and I also ate till our stomachs could fill. And thus, that there was hardly left anything for the girls, just cleared everything off. Then, the girls had brought some videos, unfortunately, on inspiration, so we were forced to watch them, still it was fun and we would comment something really funny during the videos. For every pre-tee, experiencing something unexpected is awe-inspiring and wild. And as we ever could have had any expectations of fun from the ortho-egoist, this party was really something special. And hence, we went completely cracked that day. 'Rave-Rejoice-Repeat' that's what we did.

The feeling that day was something else. Like some kind of revolution had occurred in the ortho-egoist's heart, mind and soul. Ever been so pissed off by the work load and bored so much that the mind is suffocated and then suddenly by someway you get a week off, that is the happiness felt after hearing about the party.

The party idea was really human of her, truly kind. Hats off to the ortho-egoist. Believe it or not, that morning all classmates found a emotional touch from the teacher. Conclusion: Our teacher is bitter not bad. And bitter things are required to get us immune. But inside her bitterness lied a sweet core.

Her insults may be the worst abuse we might get from a teacher, but this party idea just wiped her pathetic nature. And I guess those insults will make us ready to hear badly from the bosses in the future.

That make me learn that pre-teens are those stubborn mules that have to be given proof for everything. Because the word 'why' jams the whole brain. And also that pre-teens don't believe in anybody easily. And that's because they believe that what trust can only bring is tears and bloodshed (exaggeration). But the party was adequate evidence to prove goodness of the teacher and thus, we understood that she ain't bad.

She might be and most probably is the scariest, sternest teacher of middle school but that's ok, until she does such works of good till the end. Such attitude taught me something, if you always fulfill everybody's wish, then one might get prodigal, but if you just fulfill the requirements, the one might become a prodigy. Prodigy and prodigal have a small difference in spelling but vast in it's meaning: prodigal is being spoilt, and prodigy means being a genius.

So don't always pamper everybody by giving all resources, or being the nicest guy, instead give few slaps when one asks for more than what he requires.

After all, everything that happens is the gimmick from the human mind.

THE NAME-FAME GAME

Middle school is really a place to be, but only when you are keen on fighting for recognition. Everyone wants fame, the power of identity is much more wanted then some lousy A grades. The power of authority is of great importance. Pre-teens want stardom, for much to do, like to show-off to those archrivals, or to impress that somebody, or to just provide some extra amenities to friends, and yeah of course the biggest merit is that we can legibly, officially bunk classes.

In middle school, to acquire this power, this responsibility, this name, there are many ways, like helping teachers, being the PET, or get good marks, but these are slow and a bit tough jobs (you can't give service to anybody!!), so the faster and easier method, as we see it, is house captain elections. They are like the ATM machines to acquire fame. They give us the ability to fly high, a chance to rule, a choice to lead, and obviously the pride. Once elected, the whole year we have the power to do everything and anything, we get name and respect.

We can just flock in the corridors whole day by giving some lame excuse of completing some kind of duty, that way, we can actually bunk some boring periods. Rivals who always try to outsmart us in everything, with such power, we can easily outwit them. So, basically fame is a monopoly played by us, and that's what you love to do in middle school. I mean the peculiar pre-teens love to do. We never get entangled in any problems once elected and teachers would never know that we were the once who played the pranks. The students follow our word. We are like watch dogs, but not like the watchman who just snore outside the ATM, but the supervisors who have a check upon their employees. It's a hell of a responsibility ride but comes fun packed and action sacked. So, being a house captain is an elite post that I guess every peculiar pre-teen would want.

Nikhil, the smartest guy in my house and I wanted to participate. And there was heavy competition between us. Even though we are best of friends right now, those days were filled with jealousy and competitiveness. But I guessed that my win was easy because people would vote for me more as I was fun loving.

I thought that the elections would be easy, just throw some damn speech with long bombastic words to impress the teachers and some fake promises to impress the real 'vote bank' the students. And with the voting thing, it's an easy win. Just threaten all boys to vote, and promise all girls a candy after win, then use flattery before teachers, and all such crap.

And for the record, every time in any damn elections, the candidate with smartness in speech, wisdom in work, and some politics in promises wins over candidates with patriotism in their nerves, or discipline in their mind, or punctuality in everything so, I guess I had some good chances because of my cool and calm attitude.

They say, for every big task, you need some contacts, and I would say that that statement is correct, because whatever what ability might be, you will always get a place somewhere because of networking. So, with the smartness I possessed, I also had my nice impression on the head of our house. With that, my confidence got some more thrust.

There were just kids up for the elections, and from those, one would reach the cloud nine and the other five would be just dumped. Turn by turn, everyone gave speeches; some were good, while some just gave their bio-data. Everyone wanted to catch as many hearts as they could with the only promising words they had.

As I told, for me, from all the 5 others, the real competition was Nikhil, a frenemy who was with me during the last years, he used to boast about his talent all the time. He was talented, skilled but was egotistical. If his ego were removed some way, I would definitely vote for him. He spoke fantastically and for a moment, I thought he will win for sure.

Just a tip for every stage fearing pre-teen (almost all), that after giving any performance, if the crowd doesn't respond well, that's because they are just too lethargic, just ignore them, and if you think you aren't confident enough because you are afraid of criticism after the show, don't worry, because middle school critics are just those punks who actually can't do anything. People always throw rocks at things that shine.

And you cannot ever expect a standing ovation from the pre-teen crowd. Even light claps from few non-depraved souls are enough. And this practice of not motivating others is because they are drunk of jealousy. Don't ever complain, because then they will ready the coffin and the pit for your talent.

When everyone had spoken, the girls and the boys, it was time for results. We were pretty sure that the winner was either my frenemy or I. Either I took the cake or the ball was in his court.

And then after calculating the votes per each candidate, there were about 200 voters, the ambience of that place was changing fast, pressure in everyone nerves, heat from all corners and sweat on the collars and the temple. The gossips got louder, but we acted like normal, we both dumbasses were over-confident about our win, and what happened next was just jaw dropping and spit falling. It froze everyone's blood and veins.

As the teacher finished her job, and stood up for announcing the result, for a second all heartbeats stopped and then again they started beating fast and loud accompanied by tense. "And the house captain is" with that coming out of the mouth, we both almost stood up, but then she took the name of some unknown guy, someone about whom we hadn't heard of. We were all shocked with our mouths as big that could fit an adult dragonfly. We were literally bewildered. No word for it.

I thought that it was a joke, but it wasn't. Some anonymous getting such post; such power; OMG. Our efforts were crushed and the chocolates I had brought to give everybody who voted for me went in vain. And we had lost against whom, a naught, a nobody, OMG. We were like 'what the!?!' Nobody, the candidates or the spectators could believe what their ears heard or what their eyes saw. Completely blew us.

And the other fact was that everyone in the crowd was supporting me. the boys and most of the girls. Some fanatics turned wild and reacted obnoxious, aggressive. Everyone started opposing the decision. Had they elected blindly, without comparing the attributes, the style, the passion, just messed my mood completely. The boy who was selected didn't have any experience, he was a year younger to me and maybe a century younger than my brain. That puny little nerd, just took the cake into his mouth.

Now, that made me learn to never expect something expected from school, because they are habituated to give the unanticipated. There are no logistics based on what someone decides something in middle school.

People say, that if we are confident enough, we get whatever we ask for; but to apply that ideology in middle school is the biggest mistake one can make. So, whenever you are damn sure about your win, don't get carried away, because losing awaits your destiny. Middle school is just too shocking, never expect anything out of it that will give you all the gold and wine.

Expect the UNEXPECTED.

That was one hell of a backstabbing move by the teacher. A fair lose s okay for any pre-teen, but bias decisions are like injustice for him. Giving someone else power and reputation just wasn't right.

The only way to resolve the confusions and to dissolve the inner agitations, there was only one way that was to confront the teacher. Asked a simple question, 'what was in him, and not in me?', and waited for an answer.

Loosing to an enemy because he was a bit better is okay and gives more thirst of winning the next time, the next challenge but loosing because of some kind of foolish fallacy just stops us from participation the next time. But, I took the decision for fighting again, I am not going back.

Ma'am gave an answer, it was satisfying but way too complicated. She said that there were two reasons, the first one was that she couldn't elect the house captain boy and girl from the same grade because of the school norms, which felt complete bullshit to me. They should see the talent not the standard, for Christ's sake.

The second reason was acceptable, it was that she didn't wanted any advancement in the rivalry between me and the frenemy, because she thought that win of someone from us two would spark more enmity, would increase more jealousy and upsurge more competition in us. And the teacher didn't want that to happen because that would bring bad outcomes onto us and also create too much bad blood between us.

And it is thoughtful as long as it is true, because gaining friendship could be better than fighting like cats and dogs, and chasing each other's post as mice and cats. Enjoying a strong bond is better than being 'someone'. Sympathetic thinking from the housemaster.

But, at the same time, getting the knowledge of my loss, I was disheartened as my dream of becoming famous was shattered like a hammer would do to a castle of glass. My goal to reach a post with glamour and reputation was crushed, and though the reason behind it was not evil still it was biased, they shouldn't have done that.

I was really angry. Kapil and Aditya came to make me calm and all, but I guess their efforts were going to go in vain. They told me that our school never knew how to honour the right students and that inter politics is what leads to such decisions. But I didn't wanna listen them, because on the inside the beast was rising, the demon awakening, I was really angry as hades that day. No matter what anybody said, I could not resist this decision and would burn like hell inside. I felt like a fallen angel, let down. And then after hours of inner cry and Kapil's tries to stop me from abusing school system and Aditya's all attempts to cease me from going down and trying to build up my self esteem and self confidence again, I stopped. But still I couldn't understand their name fame stupidity.

I mean, are they playing a game, a name-fame game, because if they are, I ain't having fun, and for the record, if they want to continue these games then even I am not interested in this shit; let school get wrecked, I don't care.

But who is it played? Is it I being moved on the game tracks, or is the boy selected getting paid as a marquee player? This is getting complicated, so I decided to forget all of it, but I also decided not to anticipate for anything before hand. What I learnt was that, whatever happened, true or false, such elections or probably more apt is politics is no good for us. We are too immature to face this phase and fall into such trap of responsibilities.

Pre-Teens:
learn new things

Cheat
TRICK
• POLitiCs↑

politician

bogus
Tales

Dreadful

Emotionally Retards

AstroloGer

FRIDAY
13

(darkest... day of my Life)★

♥ Stupidity ♥

Philanthropist...

The Real Filth Of Middle School Shows Up ....

nonstop - nonsense...

abc→zyz

Crazy

collegish

C R
H S U

cello

Billionaire PlayBoy

Love - thing

*rumors

Dreams

nightmare

Genius

THE REAL FILTH OF MIDDLE SCHOOL SHOWS UP

After entering pre-teenage, we learn many things, some good-some bad. We learn about the politics played by the school, we learn about new methods to cheat, trick. Well, sometimes we also learn the fact that there is one more gender in the world. Well, those things are okay and normal and affectless but what is the main problem is that we start pretending like teens even though we aren't. our talks turn college'ish'. Whereas some pre-teens add asterisk to every sentence in their speech. And a few start becoming astrologers, stupid astrologers.

Eh? Did I say an astrologer? The one with wicked vibe on and that funny torso and pajamas with stars and moons printed on them in silver. The one who covers his barbarous Afro hairstyle with a hood. The wimp who has those cards that tell you your future that is mostly wrong.

Oh yeah! Those money magnates who lie and just hoodwink everyone in their stupid magic and some old wives' tales. The person who uses his abilities to manipulate our feelings and force us to be oppressed every time. The stories that they speak, after collecting a huge amount as fees, are those bogus tales; they say that they can decide our future and mold our destiny, as if they are gods! LOL! So what does that pathetic idiot have to do with our pre-teenage, I mean he is a freak show, and middle school ain't for the likes of them. Not someone who can be related with a pre-teens life?

Ok, so the relation is that in our school, there are some students who pair up two boys and girls and tell about their future, and that's the dumbest and stupidest thing I have ever heard. Well, they say they are being logical and practical, which is completely mental.

So, this practice is termed as pairing. And it's the most rotten practice of all, smelly, stale and sour. It is, no doubt, the real filth of middle school.

So basically, pairing is like the 'theory of relatively' but with a twist, it ain't pertaining to physics but chemistry. Pairing is like a false relationship between 2 people of opposite sexes.

As people create religions, they create such relationships, just one different kind of act with someone of different sex, and ta da, you are a god! Well here, you are the center of all gossips. It is the most dreadful trap of all, fall in one and get lost forever in it.

In my class, almost everyone was into it, but few just would spread this while some created such fallacy. Help a person fro opposite gender, rock the stage on talent hunt day, crack a joke that's 'really' good, comment regularly during all periods, bring medals or certificates or even Nike shoes and lo and behold! You have been successfully paired with ABC or xyz girl.

For few morons, pairing was a part-time job, a time-pass a hobby, and the only sad truth is that everyone was passionate to do it. It was maybe the only thing they did seriously. They find it entertaining and amusing, but I find it completely non-sense. Playing with somebody's feelings is not a thing a pride. They say it's fun and harmless, but I never anything to laugh about, and this has led to serious differences between people, there cannot be a bigger injury than a hurt heart.

Well, every peculiar pre-teen has his/her secrets, his or her bad times, accidental incidents, to be forgotten moments, to be erased flashes of life, and maybe every unforgettable and sad minutes are the ones who fill the hearts with sorrow, and they all start here, in middle school. The root to all such gloomy episodes of pre-teenage is this pairing thing, the real filth of middle school.

Even my Friday the 13th came, the darkest day of my life, when I was paired for the first time. And then followed some 73 days of limitless teasing, criticism, sarcasm and mockery by those lunatics giving me a miserable time. They say that I have a rock heart, I don't get too much of the touchy-feels, but when we get paired, even such rocks get burned to ashes.

So the story begins with a classroom, full of happiness and joy, because of the jokes I create. I was the class clown, responsible for everyone's laughter. Everybody liked my liveliness, my chivalry, and my sociability. My stupid arguments, comical comments and droll jokes were ever awaited. Even teachers liked my frank character, my quick wit, and my *hazirjawaabi*.

Everyone likes appreciation. Everyone likes to be the charm, the main focus of the class. The thirst and the greed of having stardom were complete. I was the favourite, everyone wants to become the Iron Man of the class, as you know the GENIUS BILLIONAIRE PLAYBOY PHILANTHROPIST.

I received my share of stardom, my jokes didn't had any expiry date and were spread like wildfire. The basic talent I had was that I could give everybody a good laugh, a giggle, or even the tiniest of a smile.

So, that times were good, even though I wasn't the house captain, still I got my share of fame, I was really relishing life with that middle school class. I got ATTENTION.

Everyone wanted to sit with me, befriend me, and then share their heart with me. They wanted to share their likes, dislikes, their secrets and lunchboxes.

I was like the talk of the town (class) now, my good knowledge, soft speech got me great deal of good will. That time felt like being in a Jacuzzi on the top of a private yacht with no one else but friends. Until, a huge storm came, the real filth of middle school showed up, pairing knocked my door.

Keshav blasted into our class in recess and told me what was going on. He said that everywhere they are saying that I am in with that girl and all. Well, at that moment I was just shaken. Nothing can be as bad as being framed in middle school.

Well, I did not get into this 'love thing' at all, what had happened was that few morons, the 'emotionally retards' paired me up with a girl, I mean, that's crazy, how can you call simple communicating, joking or complimenting in any heck way flirting? And they did think like that. They judged me as if they knew about me. Idiots. And so I was in a fix, paired up with a girl who I hardly knew, and then started the sarcasm. This happened with not only me but also others, like J.D. (Jay Desai) was paired up with a girl which was like a sister to him, Nikhil got into the gossips when he was paired with a girl that was just in the same tuition classes which Nikhil went to. And then there were sarcastic comments, cynical laughs and all sorts of mockery.

Whenever I was near that girl, almost 4 feet from, I would see everybody coughing that was like an indication about our pairing; or whenever I would talk with her, it felt like valentine as some lunatics would have surrounded us like cupids, this was completely insane.

Well, the bigger worry was that these people spread this talk all over, and pairing thing spreads like wildfire. So my life started bugging me again, it felt too annoying.

Not only those punks, but few friends of mine also started teasing and spreading this, those backstabbing devil; and every time anyone did that to me, I would say, "stop this non-sense, you stupid astrologers". The first friend to back-stab me was Ishaq and Anuj. They literally told about this bogus story to every single person they met. This was now the talk of the class.

Well, I also learnt something, that is to never trust anybody, as a devil dwells in also the purest of hearts, and you don't know when he can show up. And it did, the devil took me completely unawares pushing me into the ditch. I was really taken aback by such insolence by my school siblings. Such incidents of pairing are worse than even the harshest of the accidents because body isn't lost but heart is. People say that the inner strength controls the outer body, like software and hardware. The software commands, designates, thinks, and the hardware gives the output. So if this inner strength is hurt, then the whole body is affected, your body language changes, your smile vanishes, your stress and sweat increase. One tip: maintain inner might.

Ultimately, what I get to know is that my mixing attitude, my attitude of adjusting, and my adaptation techniques and of course my flashy eyebrows brought me this trouble: pairing, the worst predator that preys emotions. But does that mean, I had to stop being me, or I had to stop being my attitude. Not happening!!

Well, as they say, to get something popular enhance the marketing of a product, those maniacs started that too. Those astrologers brought some pathetic new methods to make me sadder than ever.

My story, my pairing tale was broadcasted on every news channel of those astrologers, i.e. said and repeated by all those thugs.

And then they came up with some new abbreviations, which were really meaningless. So what they did was took a famous company's abbv. And then replaced the worlds with some college'ish' words pertaining to love and relationships, and these abbv. were used to tease someone who was teased. Like reliance became relationship, limited became love, public became Prasham, or retail became Ritesh, or jade became Jay. It was something completely rubbishes and for me it was something to be down into the bin. And then we were criticized by those heartless beats, now that's something that CAN bring frustration. It was kind of a special attack by those freaks to me us feel even more low, and we did.

Everyone who was paired had to face this shit, this pairing thing getting to some other extent, making us all numb inside out; burn inside out.

Besides this abbv. method, they also had another 'nuclear' weapon which was big, destructive, heart-breaking weapon, it was 'the rumours'. The worst that has ever happened to middle school. That's what powers and motivates evil in middle school, actually half of the activeness in middle school is because of this, and pre-teens love spreading something that never exists.

Rumours, they are something that can fire water, vaporize almost everything on the periodic table, turn anybody's life upside down, they got the power to take away all sorts of positivity in anybody. Highly hazardous.

What are they, basically? Well, to find a perfect and ideal answer to that, is like an impossible thing. What answer I would provide is nuts, actually salted nuts. They are the structural and functional unit of every gossip in middle school. Their main function is to spread some kind of misconception really fast, like fire in the woods.

Ever heard of mass media? The sources who give you news, actually gives the whole world news, well rumours are the second cousins (maternal) of mass media, the only difference being that rumours spread something wrong in the worst way thinkable relating to some illogical and stupid topic (mostly pairing).

One day came, when I was really fed up, sad, tired, low by such mocking by those lunatics who had paired me, but I and a few other friends who had been paired too decided to knock those punks off by getting this reckless thing an 'adult supervision', so we went to a teacher who had complete trust in us as we had in her. And she helped through this thrones journey, she removed the essence of pairing from our life. She was a real altruist, thank god she came to our rescue

Because, with this coupling thing on, school felt like jail, I felt as if turned to ashes, losing my character and my attitude and my wide alien smile. This insolent act done by those wimps just snatched my happiness, pick-pocketed my goals of life, sidelined my jokes and just kidnapped my will asking for a ransom that couldn't be paid. I became emotionless, and the smile that had gone away won't return.

In Pre-teenage, a moment of joy, triumph, victory, friendship, love, respect can give satisfaction and meaning to life as these small things convey the hidden message, the forgotten purpose of having a normal and happy-go-lucky life.

But a rumour, a foolish act, a big mistake, a backstabbing friend and obviously pairing can topple this castle of happiness, can turn the tables. It can make life, nothing but hell. Happiness into regret. It can change our vivid 4k colourful life into a pitch-black void of emptiness. It can change your naughty, unconditioned smile into a fearful, worthless frown. It can crush your life of dreams into a fortress of nightmares.

TRANSITION: FORGET THE PAST AND RESTART ROCKING

This big bump on my flawless pre-teenage just put me in a fix. It was something really awful. But, then I stopped for a moment, and took a decision that it was time to forget the past, and start over again. It was high time now to be in the past lost in a limbo. It's time to set new milestones, bet new risks, and let the good times roll. The stakes are now high, and I can't be living in the past, because living in the past is like doing a suicide from the real life. So being in the real world is what I got to do, otherwise have some patience for someone taking me to a morgue. I have to regenerate activeness and liveliness in me.

I made a resolution that day though it wasn't 1st Jan, that I had to leave the pairing incident down the road, people are strange and jealous, so whatever stories the world makes, I shouldn't get affected, so I am not stopping my success story here. I should start making my mark now, stating typing my legend, because once it starts it cannot end, and like that inspiring myself I spit out the worries.

If every pre-teen starts to take such resolutions and decide his fate, then I guess success isn't hard at all. The only thing that matters in life is a promise, and the strongest of the promises is the one made to oneself.

And that very moment when I took the resolution, I wiped my tears and also my bad memories, took the pairing thing and dumped it into the bin, left all the selfish friends with nothing but guilt, rebooted my emotions, refreshed my mind, cleaned my heart, and started afresh.

The only thing I didn't want to change was my attitude, and that's because nothing can change your attitude as it inimitable, plus there are no copyrights to copy anyone's attitude.

Okay, I admit, I was a nut case, some even said I had a spoiled attitude but sometimes people don't understand the uniqueness and peculiarity of someone's attitude, they feel that they are the only ones right. So, everybody take your attitude as your special dish, never change it on somebody else's order, modify according to your needs, your choices.

Now, as I had resolved to change my present by forgetting the past, I needed a transition to transform my mood from gloomy to glistering. Deleting the bugs and removing the errors, the first phase of transition had started. I called it the 'recover phase'. Then removed the frowns to bring back the clown in me.

Done. Done. Done. The to-do list of the first transition phase was over. Next on the checklist was to subtract the selfish and 'I' oriented people, and then add some new friends, find some new people to guide me, assist me and accompany me. I needed real friends. I now no longer wanted to be with people in disguise of friends or the ones who wore the masks of friendship but were enemies in real.

To have faith in somebody is much more than respecting somebody, and after going through all that crap, I hardly could trust anybody. Finding friends is like finding a needle out of the haystack because out of 9 billion people on earth, not everybody is genuine and friendly. Anybody could turn out to be a fugitive.

After lots of hard work, and bunks, and all the flocking in the corridors, I found some people who could be the ones. The besties. I found three people in whom I saw the desire for friendship.

The first was a normal, simple, 'knows everything' type of guy, having medals hit the drawers at his house, simplicity in his blood. He could think lateral, but above all, he respected the might of true friendship.

The next one was a pure *Punjabi*- moody, short-tempered, ever-happy, amateur, but having lots of potential. He was the most frank and sweet kid I had ever seen.

The last one was a nut case, the last monkey of our gang, he was the creator of all problems but was the one who used to solve them for us, was into the school politics, had great imagination and was crazy.

We never had any confidence over anyone of us, still some secret power of trust kept us along, and because of our infinite pranks, we called ourselves 'the Vandalism Viceroys'.

75

That's it for the second phase of transition, making friends, the best thing to do in life. They completed me again, helped me get past the dark void created by pairing.

I was back into the fun business. I forgot the past and decided to restart rocking. Pairing = history. My new friends devised a new reply for me to give it to every idiot who teased me; now whenever someone tried to annoy me, I would say, "hey blockhead, are you drunk, drunk of jealousy, that you are so busy in pissing me and my talent off", and that worked perfectly.

The next big thing happened to me was that I stopped playing all those bad pranks, and for some reason started respecting everybody. Studies gave me enjoyment and my mind was no more distracted to do monkeyshines. What is the transition that had brought such maturity.

Or else, I would be found busy on sticking gum on everybody's hair, or pouring oil in the gap between the chest and the shirt of boys, or dirty everybody's trousers, or ink those Thursday white shoes. But this maturity had changed me.

No pranks from now on. That's good for people who don't like them. Troubles were now troubleshot. Oh yeah!

My charisma returned back, my personality checked in, my frowns vanished, my sadness was now history, my new friends rocked my new life and the best thing was that the pranks went oblivion.

I felt dancing and galloping and jumping because now life was in motion. A life with no ups and downs is bland, no movements show nothing but death (even on ECG). So, preteens next time you get a bump, just leap over it. Enjoy life as if it were to end tomorrow and live life like you were never going to die. Be happy, that's all you need to be. A life less enjoyed like a squeezed lemon.

The transition phase really helped me escape the land of sulks to the islands of smile. Its time to relax, I have time, I have my heart and I have friends, that's all I would want currently. Rejuvenation. Freshen up. I felt like I was on the top of the world, it felt like spring and sprung and my new life had shone. Transition was turning out to be a nice period. Rocking restarted.

But again the problem started. I had stopped all the pranks, and still few people worth naught complained about me, only because jealousy.

On my side, I have got courage, bravery and might and experience; what do they have? Some kind of stupid excuses, or 100-year-old (metaphor) stories about me that are now nothing but history, or fake complains. Lets see what happens!!

THE DRAMA QUEEN DOMINATION

As I said, few of the nitwits started to complain about me every time, even those times when I was as innocent as Mary's lambs. So for a moment, I was really getting pissed off. I mean, even though I didn't commit any crime, or did any prank, then why so much heat upon me? It seems as if I am the one blamed, the *GABBAR* for everything.

Okay, I understand that the number of pranks and their intensity had increased. And that's because now the pre-teens weren't afraid of teachers nor were the even the slightest worried about the consequences they would face once they were caught. And if you see, that type of courage is pretty lame and lousy.

The new generation is oddly talented, peculiarly talented, they had all the abilities, but believe me, and they use it on the negative hemisphere more. The pre-teens of today had snap judgment. They just got some spooky idea of a prank from somewhere, collected all the ingredients, crossed out all on the to-do list, and then did it before thinking twice. Cool, right? Wrong. They disturbed the teachers and made someone cry with high-pitched shrieks.

But they never got entangles in any problems as everybody had the blaming power. So all they needed to do was finish off the prank and then blame the nerds, dirty everything and name some anonymous kid. That is the basic psychology of every peculiar pre-teen.

The blame game would set course to many problems, it would give many aftershocks in the middle school and would leave the last person blamed by the blame chain in a hoax. I mean there was no way out for the last blamed person to show his innocence.

The bigger worry to me was that the last person blamed was me, and that was because before I was hard-core prankster, so the teacher would think it was me, even though I wasn't the one. And so the monitors would grumble about me, the girls would always moan, and many others would protest leaving me in the prison with my innocence and goodness sidelined and silenced and overruled. So even though I wasn't guilty, they put me on the guillotine.

This monopoly had to be stopped. Monopoly? Oh yeah, it was their control over the class, and we were being wrecked like servants, whereas they enjoyed like big fat lethargic bosses. Because I cannot forever face the heat, my butt's not free for spanking nor are my cheeks. Clearly unfair.

Then I understood, that it was my mistake, I should never have tolerated, never have digested the scolding, I could have spilled the truth. If I pity them then I am being cruel to myself. And as always, self before service gives faster fruits. Okay not always, sometimes listening to elders, we should serve before self, but it always depends. If the actions could be pre-determined then there would be no term as 'confusion' or 'hitches' nor would there be so much thirst for solutions.

Got it! The key to unlock myself rom the prison where I have been kept as a fugitive. I got to complain about the real pranksters, truth always finds it path. I got my ticket out of this plethora of problems. Got my way to reveal the real sinister imps. My chance to 'grumble'.

Then was my turning point, to decide what to do. I concluded that the next time I was blamed I would directly go and protest about this. It was my chance to stop thinking ten times before acting, next time this happens and I would fire a shot. I was sure to bedazzle the losers, 'cause this time I was going to be the winner. My determination was bejeweled by my confidence.

Next time they decided to trap me into this labyrinth, and a week later, I got my opportunity, the perfect moments to try my idea out. The scenario was like that, the class lunatics had done serious chalk fights in the class, turned the class actually powdered the class into a forest. Just white. Boom. The class was all covered in chalk bits, the windows as if tinted by the chalk powder, and as the teacher entered the class, we were sure it would sure be a battle cry, as the monsters of the class had turned the class upside down.

On asked, with anger and rage, everyone pointed me out, even though I was innocent. What the heck is this? A conspiracy. A sedition. A treachery. They surely needed a lesson.

I was innocent. And prepared, without hesitation or any kind of pity or mercy for them I went to the teacher, said her the whole story, my friends came to my support, leaked all information about the nuisance the lunatics were creating. I told the teacher that the lunatics were trying to cheat the teacher and escape.

Confident?......yeah!

Afraid?............ nah!

Cool?........hell yeah!

Spilled out all about the blame games they had played before and how they entangled me. So, the only action ma'am could do was to call all wimps and scold, hit, slap, whack, smack, or thwack them. On called, the nitwits were gonna be hanged, that's what I thought, but what happened was the opposite of it. Instead of ass-kick the morons, the morons with kick-ass 'making up things' power spun some other superficial yarn.

As the lecture of the teacher started, the all very emotionally impaired idiots started whining and sobbing, they were literally flowing rivers out there. Real big crocodile tears. The lecture half finished stop and then all they got is some stupid sympathy and a cheap advice.

So basically, those tears made me and my idea sink deep, drown down the failure sea. Sorcery, a big sorcery. The teacher not at all understood their drama.

They got no punishment, that's injustice to me. Not even a slap, or a 'sophisticated' note in some freaking last page of any stupid notebook. And all they got to pay was some bargained NaCl. These people, that day got a title from me, the 'drama queens'. Because only their stupid saltwater bailed out the problem, not my truth, or the evidences I presented.

So, that meant I had to pay for their sins. They are surely in debt. @#$%. Emotional blackmail. That's what they excelled in.

So they were the emotionally retarded who aimed emotionally mediocre people like me and other normal (usually male!!) people to rule out our impression or our talent in front of teachers by using their emotionally obsessive techniques. Those typical drama queens. They were of many types, some were sophisticated, some were selfish, and some were naturally, while many were weirdoes. All drama queens.

Here it started! The domination of the drama queens. Do all kinds of peccadillos, create all kinds of confusion, enrage everybody, turn anybody's life upside down, do pranks and make a fool out of anybody, fashion hell but then always escape with simple dramatics including just few tears, filmy dialogues and that expressions. Not everybody's cup of tea, but the maestros get unlimited merits.

If we did the emotional blackmail, then we would be defined as small cranky and stubborn infants, whereas their cried would be HEARD. Drama queens were real fraudsters, they would pull a heist of pranks and escape by the blame game or serious sobbing. They were cheap jerkidos, actually cheapest.

Well, it was not only injustice to us students, but also a betrayal for the teacher. You cannot act so selfish, and cry every time if something ain't your way. That's off the pre-teenage rulebook. Sheer nonsense.

The drama queens were really coming out to be a pain in the butt. And unfortunately, almost everybody got into this business. Today's generation doesn't want to do good. *'ganda hain par dhandha hain! Kya kare?'*

Foxes they were, actually vixen. Shy actions with sly mastermind. Utterly malicious. This business would give great profits, but it wasn't worth it, 'cause it wasn't ethical according to pre-teenage living standards.

Another characteristic of those characterless freaks was that they could not digest the teacher praising somebody, and then would get into the process of ruling such students off the whitelist.

But then, I also realized that such people were necessary; even after facing such harsh heat of their domination, something kept telling me that they were integral for right grooming of pre-teens.

They might be vexing our lives, ruining in some cases; might me putting tar on our success story but sometimes such experiences teach us a lesson; always remember, tar provides good roads, well this might give a smooth success path. The drama queens taught me and all other irked a lesson that selfish people can ruin our lives but if we recognize the method of solving their tantrums and regenerating their calm then life would as easy as ABC.

They add that special lime to our cocktail; they add petrol to our inner fire; they might be something hazardous, but now a days, it's important to get immunized.

One tip: get immunized to the drama of such people, get vaccinated to the vexing of people, get prepared to face the domination by those selfish morons, or else get sidelined with **facepalm** getting hallucinated by the sunstroke from the heat of the drama queens.

BUTTER V1.0

After the drama queens' domination, we all good ones were off the whitelist. They had literally spit out our impression and now the teachers' mind was filled with some false filth uploaded by the blackmailers. We were now known as the ill-mannered, spoiled, ruthless students whereas they had now achieved free respect. Our white collar was now inked black.

A pre-teen loves respect, good will, admiration but above all stardom. His fame might be out of nothing or out of limitless sweat and time; it also might also be as an outlaw or a simple butler; it can also be of simple adulation (flattery) or through extreme hard work. Anyway possible, because all he needs is recognition, fame and wants to be in the limelight on the stage, then that's by long surnames or big pay cheques; or some cheap flowers; or with honesty and hard work; hook or crook, it doesn't matter until he is cloaked in the fame suit.

Fed with bad remarks, we were no longer in those shiny bright eyes of the teachers, and that really moved us. Demoralized us. Which made us get a new honorific, that's those prefixes like Mr. or Dr. or Mast. Well our new honorific was 'notorious', it was first 'renowned'. Now there's a need of a remedy. Serious stuff to be done. Big project to do. Drama queens snatched our pride, fame and marks too. Bandages don't fix bullet holes. The best remedy would also fail in diminishing this cut.

Drama queens were now getting attention, freakingly good attention. We needed a meeting to scout for a new solution. In the summit, we chatted about the methods of the rule. After a lot of research and development (that's basically debating over what's better: drama queens or rivals.), craft and graft (that's bringing new ideas and fusing them to create one BIG thing), formulae and algorithms (that's getting the right intensity and planning of the BIG thing) we found the solution to outwit, outthink, outnumber, outface, and outsource the theater empresses. We came up with 'BUTTER v1.0'

What is BUTTER v1.0? Well, it isn't exactly butter, not even something edible. That's something of high technology with sweet words, compliments, soft-spoken melodies, and all sorts of wrong praises, basically it's concentrated flattery lotion type of thing. Apply it on teachers and win their appreciation, become the favourite jut by saying two good words for her. Well, the profit is that even when you don't like somebody, or have that bad blood, you can have it smooth by winning his or her hearts by using this tool. To get back on the whitelist and stable our impression, we need to use it extensively. All you need from your side are concerned eyebrows, emotions, and compassionate eyes, and of course a fair budget to buy all those cards and roses for the teacher to be flattered.

Everyone was moved by this idea and now it was the in thing. Everyone did this. It was kind of a revolution to stop the monopoly of the drama queens. Due to which for a moment, the coordinator thought that we pre-teens had got some etiquettes (impossible).

But still, here lied a hierarchy, as the impact of BUTTERv1.0 was not always the same. The effect of it was different on the teacher depending upon the student. Some were the champions of using it whereas others lacked the patience and had temper problems. Some were good but irregularity and laziness hindered their path. Whereas some didn't needed to use excessive, as a skyscraper of impression was already created on the teacher by the elder sibling.

So measuring the influences of the flattery, students were ranked into three groups, based on the adulation power of the individual; based on the output received from the input given. The lowest ones on the list were the 'flattery slaves'; they tried hard but because of their 'issues' with specific teachers. The middle ones were the slavery wizards; they had power greater than all but not that conviction the rule flattery. The most influential were the 'flattery kings'; they made into the blue-collar list, and also the whitelist with their extra-ordinary control over their adulation prowess. They had unlimited resources to please the teacher. Whole day, all-day they would flatter. Topped the list, the hierarchy order.

FLATTERY SLAVES
- SHORT TEMPERED
- HAD THOSE *ISSUES*
- IRRITATED OTHERS
- GAVE TEACHERS GOOSEBUMPS WITH THEIR PRANKS

- USED BUTTERv1.O POORLY, TRIED HARD BUT
  FAILED TO GET THAT ATTENTION.

FLATTERY WIZARDS
- MEDIOCRE – STUDIES, ADULATION, PRANKS
- HAD SOME KIND OF SPELL TO IMPRESS
  TEACHERS
- USED BLACK MAGIC TO DECIEVE TEACHERS
- FED BAD ABOUT OTHERS AND GOOD ABOUT
  SELF TO THE TEACHER
- USED BUTTERv1.O FAIRLY

FLATTERY KINGS
- ELITE IN ADULATION SKILLS
- TOPPED THE WHITELIST
- RANKED NO.1 IN HEART
- SOFT-SPOKEN, SWEET, METICULOUS
- USED BUTTERv1.O EXTENSIVELY

Now, everyone was busy in buttering the teachers. The turbulence created was great. An adulation protocol, it seemed. Teachers were really happy getting compliments, roses, cards and proper treatment from the students. No longer was the rule under the drama queens. We got all the attention we needed.

The program went a boom. We wee no longer called the jerkidos, or the fraudsters and our old honorific was retrieved. Simultaneously, we were getting really good, I mean being good felt nice. It was not always that it's good to be bad. Sometimes a slave in heaven really feels better than being the king of hell. Something installed positivity in our batch.

ATTITUDE ADJUSTMENT, BEHAVIOUR MODIFICATION, PERSONALITY ALTERATION. Somehow, now mutual relationships started working out. Team spirit. Yeah!

We started helping girls (THE LAST THING TO EXPECT FROM BOYS, UNLESS YOU REALLY LIKE THAT GIRL), did group projects like a group. Respected everybody. Being good never felt so beautiful. Well, that was the turning point; we learnt the most important thing of life, that's- studies aren't as important as a right attitude, and once your popularity spike start, ego is your worst enemy. Help to get help, stay cool, have friends and live (the most important).

But as even moon has craters, BUTTERvl.O had its own bugs. And that was the different magnitude of attention for everyone. I mean, giving more to the kings, less to wizards and least to slaves would not be the apt thing to do. About the Kings, they no longer needed to lurk for extra marks, nor were they ever caught after any pranks, and could break all the laws but then hide with the thick butter.

We then thought that we need not needed BUTTERvl.O anymore, as now we wanted ranking on the base of calibre not flattery. And somehow thought it as sheer inequality, pre-teens can't bear it.

So we had to put a the end banner to it, flattery kings were now history, we asked everyone to stop using BUTTERvl.O and those who used were left to rot. The wizards were asked to forget their spell and leave sorcery down the laboratory. The kings were asked to unite with the moments and the slaves were sacked. Basically, everyone was asked to cease flattery to impress anybody, and do everything with whole heart and full sweat.

Even though, the journey of flattery initiative ended in the pit, it taught us two things- 1) the impact on others on being good. 2) The feeling we get if someone respects us back.

BUTTERv1.O was a great invention, but we failed to use it in limits. After ending this revolution, this programme, we turned back normal. Then, started all the activities in school, but teachers selected students on face value, so now the requirement of fame increased. And for fame, the thing you need to do is become the butler of the teacher. Next step was stepping into the fame, because staying on the ground is no longer advisable, get ready to climb.

STEPPING INTO FAME

As I said, the activities started. And that brought both order and chaos to middle school. Due to the drama queens' domination, and the flattery kings' supremacy, there was a lot of movement. Everybody was in a move to get reputation.

The middle school activists, and perhaps every other kid was ready to get soaked into to the pool of ideas to find the quickest and wittiest ways to get into limelight. It seemed as if a syringe of adrenaline was injected in pre-teens to get stardom.

What would be the condition of a place hit by floods, on the seismic zone, waiting for a hurricane to come and the volcano to erupt, to which the aftershocks could be devastating!!! Relax, there's no place like that, I am just trying to use it as a metaphor to explain you all how the middle school was, how the moments were, and how the activeness was spread. Spread like an epidemic.

Everyone was now fighting for identity, fishing for fame. I mean this is just crazy, to get so mad to be known. But people around were really 'mental asylum' types. Some wanted to repeat history like Mr Gandhi or sir Lincoln by doing something patriotic or probably political. Whereas some were so big sports

.reak that all they could dream was about Sachin Tendulkar's hair or Barcelona's home jersey. Or some wanted to become a science geek, a mathemagician, and some dreamt of rocking the ramp.

Few even had the naive idea of becoming the god of cricket, or the overlord of some other stupid topic. I mean, are there less religion in India that they want to add more?

They say, fame is a game, if you don't play it seriously, than you get played, and that would really be the doomsday of life. I mean life of fame. There were two paths before me, get fame and be the star, or leave it, live the small moments of all. Tough choice!

That's because I guess fame is not being almighty, it can sometimes cause misunderstandings and misconceptions, or influence our lives to follow the bad; or it can break true friendships or make new friends who just take benefits; it can unleash jealousy, increase agony, create confusion, and sometimes people you love start envying you. So getting a bad outcome could be upsetting.

Fame can take to places where only dreams go or turn life into the worst nightmare. It can give fun, independence, and adventure or can encage you into the prison of ego, loneliness and boredom. It can fetch you true love, respect, autographs and a sensual tuxedo or can snatch away your friends, your passion, your love, yourself, and your favourite old pyjamas too.

So will walking down the path of fame bring satisfaction to life? Will it bring good friends with whom you could watch a sci-fi movie relating the doomsday or some nice relatives you could party with during New Year? Will it help me fly towards the cloud 9? And if it turns out to be horrible, then is there a reverse gear to this rollercoaster ride?

One of the biggest choices to make, I mean in middle school, fame is okay because it's on a small scale. But the addiction to it could bring pain and sorrow or could build up the thirst and determination to reach the peak of excellence. At that moment, I faced a real standstill. Confused. Confused. Confused. And no snap judgement came to my rescue.

I mean the only thing that left me in double mind, was the risk of losing friends, something seemed wrong about the fame thing. I thought that if I took the step, would I be forever afar from my friends. But then, my friend tapping on my shoulder said that our friendship couldn't break, and I should continue on my route to fame. And that dazzled me. Like, the whole mentality that my friends would fell badly, or the ideology that my friends would be inferior and thus I would forget them was wiped off. That approval just gave me a kick-start.

Fame has always been that element that fuels every pre-teen's car; fame always gives thrill. But friendship feeds our hunger for excitement. Fame gives mental support, but friends provide emotional support.

Pre-teens, on any level, are thirsty for fame and starve for stardom. They have limitless goals and wild imagination, for which they need fame. Fame is vital but at the same time friends are important as well. Friends are the most expensive gifts from god; never ever afford to lose them.

Real friendship is not from those who wipe tears, but they are those souls whose memory makes you cry. When tears come while remembering the good old days enjoyed with true friends give, the real value of friends is revealed.

Still, I thought that fame wasn't worth it. I mean risking friends would be like backstabbing. I mean I can't fly like an eagle and leave all my friends as groundhogs. THAT would make me a nincompoop.

But hearing affirmation from friends just relieved my mind of the barrier. I decided to take this rather peculiar (like me and all other pre-teens) choice, paddled hard to reach the junction from where it starts, got aboard the fame express and then prepared myself of hitting a home run in every field I work, and get fame (autographs should be priceless), posters, and at the same time those crazy life with friends. Simple, Peaceful And Lively.

I wanted a batch on my chest pocket but also a secret invitation for a sleepover with the host's phone number in the pocket. I wanted to lead all the processions at school at the same time talk all non-sense during the dispersal prayer at school.

Now the decision was taken, no turning back. You can't have everything at once, to achieve something you must lose something. So, what did I need to do? Apparatus ready? That's the million-dollar question. How to achieve fame? How to become the famous figure of middle school?

TO-DO LIST TO GET FAME

\#   Combine FLATTERY And DRAMA

While everyone was saying that buttering the teacher for fetching attention was not legit, blackmailing to fetch power was a bogus trick. We combined both the devils, both the catastrophes.

To get famous, you need to show drama, so every 'wannabe' pre-teen should get a practice of showing countless tantrums at the same time get habituated to compliment everybody. This cannot fetch a pale of water, but can bring fame and reputation.

Flattery and drama have a magical effect on teachers. The impact is positive until you use it in limits. And also they teach us to behave nicely (that's important, after all, too much nuisance create problems).

Flattery is like Xbox 360 and drama is like kinect, throw some extra money (here, efforts) and get some combination that's great, superb indeed. And then have double the fun.

DETERMINATION, DILIGENCE AND DEXTERITY

I know all those terms are pretty big bouncers, even I found them 'big and boring' when I looked at them on the thesaurus.com app.

A strong mind to do something could be called determination. The 'I will do it, SURELY' commitment shows determination. Conviction + will gives determination. Well, some legend said that determination is what success needs.

'Diligence' another big term with a nice meaning again. Diligence is putting a lot of efforts. Doing hard work is diligence.

The fruits of diligence are sweeter than others, some morons say sweater than other, but who would want to listen to them. Constituent hard work brings success close and teaches us the style of working 12 hours in a 4 x 4 cubicle.

DEXTERITY is what god sends you with. your skills, your talent. Ignite your dexterity to become the champion.

A melange out of three would unleash fame for you, and really make you drunk of happiness.

RISK EVERYTHING

One this journey to achieve glory, in this battle to win glamour, there is no turning back, nor is there a chance to play safe or think twice before doing anything.

Hindrances are ought to make you fall, and sadly middle school is abundant of it. Take them as challenges and leap over them as cowboys would be doing in the west with their horses. All you need to do is risk everything; risk knowledge, risk resources, risk friends or even risk a few P.T periods to get fame.

Risking either teaches you what to do or what not to do. It gives better probability of winning. Higher odds. Its like share market. The profit made by risking on some unstable company could possibly make ten times profit than a 10 year FD in a lesser time. And with the wide angles pre-teen perspective, that would be the right thing to do. Risking boosts chances of winning.

But risking everything is risky. It's only good if you just want fame. If you want to be on all boats of life then risking could be something not expected.

So these were my strategies to get fame and then I could smile over it as then I could have a loaded pre-teenage. Loaded with fun, power, fame and success. What is success, btw? Well, success is when you can do more than others can and give more than others can.

Even though elections did not brought what I had expected. But, using all those strategies, I got recognition. I made through the tough road on to the smooth paths of success. I was the epicentre of everything with fame. Too Many Followers, Too Many Likers, Too Many Pokers. My status that time was- in the lap of fame.

My middle school success was really legendary (pre-teens like to exaggerate)-NO, well it was the same old repeated glory, there were too many to have passed this test of getting reputation. But my three strategies work, that means, all the readers could use it. Use them as weapons comrades to achieve triumph in claiming stardom. These rules get you into to whitelist.

So, pre-teens get ready to get your name printed in bold because once you achieve fame, all u need to do is clear the skies to embark on the journey of finding new horizons.

Getting fame should have completed me, but I did felt the absence of something. I mean, I was happy but was feeling sort of isolated. It felt as if something important was snatched away from my body.

Had I got more self-centred, or did I become to obsessive for fame? Had I forgotten the importance of true friends, or had I started being rude with teachers? I don't know, what had just happened. This feeling was creating a fire on the inside. These questions really flummox a mind of pre-teens.

Pre-teens are insane and such questions in head make them more bizarre. Being over-curios is a confusing and suicidal phenomenon for a pre-teen, because they give partial death from the real world by making pre-teens completely lost in the questions.

FAME OR FRIENDSHIP

I put all the questions aside, and then felt that such anxiety was normal for anyone who was famous. But slowly and slowly, with my ego ignited, and stress all around and that competition mentality brought by fame, I became a bit oppressive with friends and other classmates. I started feeling that I was the best, better than others.

My sycophancy (flattery) and sympathy turned to tyrannical and crude orders. And I thought that it was in the stardom business, and also the run-of-the-mill thing for everyone who was famous. That was the biggest misconception of my life (till date), and from then I wanted the rules of anarchism. So more boulder storms for my other classmates.

Now that I was a celeb in middle school, I could do a lot many things; I got to a lot many places. I could flunk classes, bunk exams, and roam in the corridors and of course take credits as well control of everything.

With great power come great responsibilities. And it did arrive. After I tasted the sweetness of power, and sipped the cocktail of fame, the dessert of responsibility showed up. And the only problem was that it wasn't worth the price. The responsibilities were in abundance like a god's mailbox, or a child's wish list for Santa.

Like the job of bringing educational videos, and teach the slow learners some chapter, and then I had to decorate the soft board, the worst of all, I had to call the janitor every time some nitwit spilled water of floor. Such works of dweebs aren't for me, I am a celebrity after all (that ego hurt me afterwards) but still, I had to do it.

I ignored the cons and focussed on the pros. It is always advisable to see the positive of everything and avoid the negatives. And on the brighter side of it, with such works I got power too, and attention as well. As every responsibility I took care of gave me perks.

I was enjoying it. The cool breeze of happiness killed the heat of worries and fear. The velocity of adventures decreased but the momentum of my success story increased. I was the cynosure (centre of talk) of the class now.

I was no longer that backbencher who would laugh like a maniac at a nerd, or play tic-tac-toe on the last page of the geography textbook, but would monitor the class; it was kind of fun and frolic. I felt like the ghost rider of class. A devil by name, helper by game and renowned by fame.

After few days, this enjoyment felt boring, it was the same routine everyday. And FYI preteens hate doing the same thing everyday. And above all, I was not feeling comfortable with all I had; I had started missing the good old days with my friends.

I guess the fame was putting barriers (imaginary) between thrill and me. I was no longer with my crazy friends. I missed them now.

Pre-teen are one of the most unexpected social animals. This beast tends to bark all day long to each and every uproar; he even gets emotional and wants to be in the pack; he likes to avenge, revenge, and scavenge through everything that contradicts him.

Pre-teens live on friends and feed on fame. The attention powers their life but friends provide the real adrenaline. They get ego, but learn Lego (nothing else was rhyming); they become selfish but for their friends they give up a lot, they get lost in the imagination but decide practically.

But the biggest truth of life is that friends can die for you. True friends. The ingredients one needs for eternal friendship is few crazy friends, non-sense talks, selfless acts, mental support and to do everything *dil se*. A true friend is the one who could pay for everybody at a restaurant without making a fuss about it, but would deny paying the 25-cent lost in a bet.

Because it's not the money that matters to him, it's the stupid replies, the funny acts, crazy helps, and a heart into everything that matters to a friend. A friend would watch the bruises and apply Band-Aids, he wont peep into your pocket and weigh your wallet. He is ready to try the spiciness of a fight between friends than the saline separation that would give more pain to the burns.

Pre-teens are berserk but that's what makes them so special, that's why the number of books on them is less, that's why people don't understand them properly. Because of their curiosity, intrigue and speciality.

After getting such popularity, I no longer could stay and play with my friends. There were no longer those senseless talks about the eating habits of some African country, or about the inventions about some handicap scientist, or about the king and queen of Bollywood because I would ignore these talks and would teleport to the auditorium for getting everything ready for the assembly. The winking stopped, the looting the tiffin stopped, the fake fights ended, all because of FAME.

The gossip in social studies was now extinct, the nonstop nonsense in science periods was now extinct, and the endless bullshit in mathematics periods was now dead, and the last bench talks in English period was now just a dumb memory. I was getting away form my friends.

I was now in a big dilemma. I was confused, perplexed, puzzled, actually I was dumbfounded. The decision I had taken was proving out to be a big mistake. Peculiar pre-teens, they always predict the output and then decide, but usually their prediction is wrong.

Plus, walking into the wrong path makes us lost and to fix the reverse gear is a hell of a task. Fame or friendship? What should I choose? Will the fruits of fame and power be more helpful than the roots of friendship? At that moment, I was really baffled!

After doing lots of research, wasting too many minutes of sleeping, and getting those drowsy eyes, the time of deciding came? Did I want to get off the fame express and go aboard the friend sedan? I never could ask for a middle school without friends, because source of entertainment is a must in pre-teenage. Fame had no value when it would come to risk friends. *REALISATION*. The fame greed had blinded.

But then, coming out of that maze, I realised that without my buddies, life would be a null void. Learnt it, indeed. Friends are the heart-winners, motivators, inspirers, and also the company-keepers. They give life hope, purpose and happiness. I had done my mistakes, so please you all don't repeat them. Because this way, getting only fame but no friends would be the apocalypse for the heart inside. Wake up.

Middle school is to enjoy life and have amusement. It is a time of endless adventures that just stun the hearts, and blow our minds. The main element of pre-teenage is laughter, and a smile is always brought by a true friend (or an enemy's failure).

Fun stands for Friend's UnioN. Greed and selfishness lead to wars and bloodshed, but friendship and fun lead to pretty crazy sleepovers. A lifetime without true friends is like a pizza without cheese, night without moon, a machine without batteries.

My mom used to say that friends are temporary and relatives are permanent. And whenever she told that, I would disagree. Friends have the same mentality, the same outlook to the world. How could they leave me? So, mom, I won't be listening to your advise this time.

But what if she is right? I mean, she was a pre-teen once, she must have been through all this. What if my friends are not what I make of them? Parents were children themselves. they might know me and my future better. But, currently, I am taking chance. I am sipping risk. I choose friends. And I will try to be with them forever.

Speeches, awards, good will, power, responsibilities, attitude, stardom give a bit thrill and delight but moments with real friends give adrenaline rush, the kick to live. Logically, etymologically, realistically, optimistically, literally or any other way friends are the closest beings to us. Be a die-hard fan of them, because they know how to reciprocate respect appropriately.

So after taking this decision of having friends over fame, I went straight to my friends, gave them a hug followed by the 'aftershock' (remember), and then gave them an apology; and after facing ignorance and oppression from, still the friends said 'no thanks, no sorry in friendship' WOW, **SALUTE***.

All readers would be and should be having such friends who don't do anything but care. Friends who just nail it! Those pals who give us those emotions when we are trying to impress someone, buddies who share even the smallest of the things they have with us, chums who give us their 'luck element'.

Fame=side-lined. Friends=primary focus. Throwing power relieved me off those responsibilities. And reuniting with naughtiness gave me a jolt. Friends should be the ones ready to make trip to hell, heaven, canteens and even the coordinators' office.

Now, middle school felt like the dome of enjoyment, in a pre-teen's life, when he gets out of some problem, when everything becomes normal, well when the atom bomb gets diffused, it becomes the best time for him. He gets the heaven effects.

Fame, fame, fame. now I guess you all must be tired of listening the same tale of fame again and again. Its' annoying, but a thing you must learn because if fame leaves you in a trance, then perhaps difficulties approach. Leaped, leaped, leaped. I successfully leaped over the fame hindrance to get back to the normal life.

The peculiarity of a pre-teen is measured in how he handles people, and how he reciprocates to other's actions. And also his wild imagination and extreme daydreaming capabilities. Remember- fame is temporary success but friendship is permanent excellence. Gifts of god, those pals are. Miss them, but don't lose them.

FRENZY FRIENDS: NOTORIOUS NIGHTS

Friendship- on. Forever. I had learnt its importance. Fun restarted. Jokes reopened. Pranks reborn. But now, as it was a long time we had talked, our topics of chats crossed the limits, we started talking on the nerds, and dweebs and their idiotic nature. Well, we knew that such talks didn't suit the teacher well. And that the complaint boxes were around. So after getting warned twice, we decided to stop it. Because we were outnumbered, as the class monitors would scribble our names in their notepads, or the complaints boxes would grumble, and what followed next was painful. Stopping it wasn't the solution, because everyday besides that topic there was nothing for us to talk about and we wanted a chance to explain the injustice done to us or share the pain we faced.

I mean friends were the only people who could understand the monopolies of lunatics and their wish to enforce their lame ideas. And friends were the only people you could sit down to find a solution to the bullies.

But with all the eavesdroppers around, we couldn't discuss this matter or else next day a blackmail would throng our inbox. That decreased the insanity, relatively.

It was rather difficult and risky to talk all these talks in school because if the person about whom were talking got to know, then four finger impression on cheeks or a shoe mark on the hip.

I could speak volumes, maybe more on any damn topic relating the negatives of middle school. But being surrounded by such environment gave us the scares. One tip: beware of them.

Blah blah blah. That's what pre-teen love doing, especially about somebody whom they envy. But never ever talk about such topics in schools because the people who surround you will be as uncertain as death. Try doing them somewhere else. Because in school those talks are explosive.

As what we wanted to express, wasn't possible at school, we decided to have sleepovers. That would be the only way to avoid the threats. Safe and secure. One tip: people would say to go on the adventurous path, but that doesn't mean you ought to walk on the minefield, think and do everything. Yup, the idea of sleepovers, that's basically go to someone's house, turn his room into a jungle, talk the whole night, empty the refrigerator.

That's the only way to release stress and share our feelings. We invited about 14 children (lucky) for the first sleepover. Everyone was excited. The host of the party was decided. All the planning and organising was done. But, on the day of sleepover just 4 of us gathered. And I am sure the other 10 are going to miss it. Kapil, Jay Desai, Aditya Kapoor and I.

It was memorable, unforgettable. Better than a family vacation in a hill station as it relieved more stress. Better than a school field trip because here we learnt new things, found solutions, scouted for more remedies. Plus, the nuisance we created having fun in our style.

We reached the host's house sharp at 8:00 pm with combed hair, tucked in shirts and a shy face (I know, what the?), and then did something even more unexpected (for a pre-teen), we greeted host's parents and grandma as if welcoming them to our weddings, with THAT respect. Somehow, our naughtiness was out and our brains could only think about the formalities like touching the feet, and removing shoes outside, and all. We felt like nerds, complete nerds. Some kind of syndrome crowded our minds about how we should behave at others' home. Afterwards, we understood that it was a right thing to do.

After all those formalities, we all signalled the host about food. We were starving (don't dare a pre-teen's appetite). And we had all thought that the food would be *'hatke'*. All four of us were heave eaters, you see. And then came the missile of disappointment, as the mother of the host said that that day they were doing some kind of fast in which they could only eat curd and vegetables. Flabbergasted, we were. And then came that 'look' on the host like bullets of a tommy gun.

As soon as we heard that no food was going to be served, we forgot the formalities, overruled the protocol, and went bananas. We excavated the whole kitchen but our efforts were in vain as all we could find were utensils and spices. Then we took over the fridge hoping to find chocolates, confectionary or maybe the whole Switzerland. But all we could find was curd, capsicums and ketchup that surely (100%)couldn't fill our breadbaskets.

Seeing this, our hunger grew, now not only mice ran, but also cats and dogs sprinted in our stomachs. And the only option left was to go to a restaurant. Because now nothing else could extinguish the flame of hunger.

The restaurant where the host took us was not too good. I mean the ambience was like some old warehouse, the air-conditioners seemed to be prehistoric and the sofa seemed to be an iceberg of foam because the upholstery was either invisible or removed. Well, such features gave us a pretty bad impression.

Still, we thought that the food quality would be good. But it turned out to be even worse. I mean, everything we ordered was unavailable or if they had it, they wouldn't have it completely. I.e- either they had breads or butter, paneer or gravy. So we cancelled everything we ordered, and just dashed out of that restaurant giving a big scolding to the manager. Disgusted.

Now, our hunger sprouted more, weird voices came out of it. We were damn damn famished. So then we walked down the road, reaching a fast food chain that was famous all over the city. And we knew it was hygienic.

The place was much better. Proper seating, proper ambience, and the food would be most probably proper. So after staring at the big menu, and getting shocked by the high prices (only the host, of course), we decided that it would be better to take the 'all-you-can-eat' thingy. Because then we could eat unlimited in limited money. The a la carte would have cost us our 3-month pocket money, combined.

It was a right decision, and the efforts of walking so much, paying much more paid off. The food was really good, the pizza was nice with sundried tomatoes adding the real flavour and the pasta were awesome with that pesto sauce combination; both accompanied by coke and our crap talks. The atmosphere there was too lively. Soothing at the same time superb.

After stuffing ourselves with too many pizza slices, relishing the hot brownie with ice-cream (included in the unlimited pack), and burping loud and stinky, we walked back to the host's house.

The sleepover had just begun, the host's room was organised (unlike most of pre-teens) but we didn't take long to turn it to one like ours. The vandalism viceroys were back to their real behaviour, mask unmasked.

We had brought extra clothes, just in case. And we changed that boring outfit, and turned into hipsters. Insanity on. We resumed the talks we had stopped at the diner. And the next three hours, we just talked and talked wildly. No sign of sleepiness, or dark circles over eyes, or boredom; we just continued. Our topics were nuts. We talked about the politics of school, the backstabbing frenemies, the bias teachers and also the mastermind and egoistical rivals. These possible talks and arguments and debates are endless on such topics, right?

1:00 a.m. have I said we four digest food very fast? so, naturally the hunger stroke back. But now where could we go. No place to have refreshments. The kitchen was hopeless. Still, we tried to find at least something, sneaking in the kitchen tip-toed and smelling every drawer like racoons. But our efforts were worthless. Challenge: lost. The midnight hunger now got wild.

Then came the bummer. As I opened the back door of the house to catch some fresh air, I saw a huge refrigerator. And to our surprise, it was full of everything. It was the golden egg. I then, gaped at the host with one brow raised and he said he didn't know anything about it. We knew he wasn't guilty for it. So, afterwards was the scenario of us eating snickers, sipping Pepsi, eating those packed nachos, and spoiling the bed. Fridge= empty. Stomachs= satisfied.

After savouring those delights, we started playing board games. I know, lame idea but I thought it could be fun with friends, but they really bored us. With nothing to do, I switched on the TV, and the only thing I could see on most channels was those teleshopping ads. Luckily, one channel was telecasting something else, and that 'else' was a bond movie.

The next couple of hours, we watched the bond movie occasionally trying to imitate Pierce Brosnan. After TV, we went to the hall, at about 3, and played Xbox.

Now, this Xbox was with kinect. The next hours, we played party games. The four of us enjoyed thoroughly. In the party games, the first one was featuring a duel in which I used to win every time. The second one was of American football, where Aditya got the most touchdowns. The third one was of bowling, and the host, Kapil was a champion of it. The last one was beach volleyball, where Jay was the best.

Till dawn, we played Xbox and still weren't at all feeling dozy. Instead our face was fresh with a glowing smile, and sweat blanketed our red face. But we had had a beautiful night. A notorious night, with such frenzy friends. One of my favourite moments of life.

Pre-teens, you should have such sleepovers because they add real spice to your life. Release your tension by such nightstays. Because, this helps you make correct bonds with the correct people. It teaches you a many things. Like how to handle a wrong turn (restaurant case) or the way of winding up and cleaning up (you got it, right?). they play a big role in providing fun to pre-teens. Plus, being with friends give excitement, wisdom and joy.

Sleepovers are the best things that ever happen to pre-teens. Esp. If with kick ass friends.

That's It

THAT'S IT

THE END, FELLAS. My book is done, now write your pre-teenage story, everyone has their own experiences, the important thing is how much you learn and enjoy in your pre-teenage, and also the number of milestones you cross; The number of hearts you win and the number of people you make laugh. Because in the end, success is about how many people remember your story.

Pre-teenage. A phase of life that is different from all and also the most crucial one as your direction is decided here. You evolve here. You transform here. Pre-teenage is the 'special effects' of your life.

Fly high from here, store those crazy moments and keep them afresh. Don't miss the small moments in it. Such small moments teach, enlighten and accompany you till the end.

My pre-teenage journey (like others) was splendid and kick ass (sometimes, ass-kick). The ups and downs giving adventure; the tunnels of darkness and haplessness continued by the broad daylight of happiness. I will miss this pre-teenage. People, please enjoy this phase and if you are reading this after your pre-teenage, then relate it with your story (I am sure you would find some similarities).

Problems galore a pre-teens life, misconceptions throng his path, making mistakes becomes routine but a pre-teen's never-say die spirit helps him cross these troubles, and their conviction and attitude always finds the right solution.

There were too many things I learnt from my pre-teenage. I would like to highlight the core points. #1 friends rock, and they stick with us. #2 teachers aren't that bad if you reciprocate well. #3 teamwork and truth wins over power of fame. These are the 3 things I learnt and I am sure that these will be with me.

Now's all the thanksgiving. I thank middle school for giving such an exciting ride; also the friends and teachers who were with me always. Thanks to my family. And special thanks to those inspirers out there who have always guided me.

Middle school had its own flaws. Everything has its 'pros and cons'. But I should say, these cons give the real thrill during pre-teenage. It can be damn good, at the same time bad.

There are billions of pre-teens, and every one of them is peculiar. Being different is the strangest thing about a pre-teen. Each one faces different troubles, each one weaves a different story.

Unique and matchless are the pre-teens. They really stun the world by what they do, how they think. One tip: never change attitude or try imitating someone else. And dream bigger dreams every time, because a pre-teen's dream is the future of the world.

Pre-teens dance lively, hear music, rave wild, party hardcore, study sometimes, enjoy eternally, get inspired, find their passion, scout for talent, polish their skills, set goals, go wild, help others, be a pain in the butt, and live life hard-core. Create new roads, don't follow the old ones. And get a wide angled perspective. And never...Never grow up! It's a trap.

Know yourself. Accept yourself. Be yourself.

And yeah! After having a superb pre-teenage, get ready to face the pimples of the next phase of life. Actually, freckles.

Next age – dream age – teenage.

Printed in the United States
By Bookmasters